Ain't We Got Fun

Ain't We Got Fun

Emily Chapman

&

Emily Ann Putzke

The
White
Rose
Press

ISBN-10: 0996385401
ISBN-13: 978-0-9963854-0-4

Published by The White Rose Press
Ain't We Got Fun
Copyright © 2015 by Emily Chapman and Emily Ann Putzke

Cover design and interior layout:
Rachel Rossano of Rossano Designs
(RossanoDesigns.weebly.com)

First Printing

Every morning, every evening
Ain't we got fun?
Not much money, oh, but honey,
Ain't we got fun?
The rent's unpaid, dear,
And we haven't a bus.
But smiles were made, dear,
For people like us!

– Ray Egan and Gus Kahn

January 1st, 1936

Dearest Georgiana,

Papa's still mad at you.

I've heard Mama crying in her bedroom every night this week. I'll look out our—well, what used to be our—bedroom window. You know the crack that's not actually cracked but is a crack somewhere inside the glass? Just as that begins to glow white from moonlight, I'll hear Papa's and Mama's voices coming from their bedroom. Donny doesn't usually hear. He's usually asleep by that time. But after awhile, he'll wake up. He always wakes up when Mama starts crying. I think their souls must be strung together by a certain bond that comes from a Mama and the Baby. Anyway, he'll wake up just as Mama's sobs begin to rattle the home-like atmosphere, and he'll come climb in my bed. He'll whisper in my ear stories. Donny's a great storyteller.

But you knew that. It wasn't so long ago that you went away.

I want you to know that I'm not mad. I don't understand why you'd leave. But I'm not mad.

Sometimes, when I lay out under the stars 'cause I can't sleep, I get a sort of longing in my veins. It stirs up my blood, and my blood trickles that feeling into my heart. Then my heart swells and swells, and I think I might burst if I don't up and run somewhere. Is that what you told me about? Is that wanderlust?

Maybe someday I'll understand you. Maybe I'm already beginning to. Maybe it's something everyone has experienced before. Even Papa. I feel like it's something that is just *human*.

Sometimes I do run, you know. When I've slipped out of the house, and everyone's asleep, and I'm lying on a hay bale in the field. When I get those tastes of wanderlust (if that's what it is), I sometimes can't control myself. I'll spring off the hay bale and go tearing through the field. It's a peculiar feeling for me. To tear through a field at midnight. For you, that would just be a mindless piece of who you are. I know it. But it's strange for me. Strangely satisfying, too. When you can't think and can only feel, run, I say. It's good for the soul.

Although I don't suggest tearing through the streets of New York City at midnight. Somehow I think the place would be too ... oh, what's the word Mama would use?

Rambunctious.

2

Be careful, Gi. Don't let anyone hurt you. Not that I expect you would. You'd glare at them with your mesmerizing green eyes for precisely three seconds. Then you'd fire a loaded pistol of words in their face and march back to ... whatever sort of place you're living in. Then whoever tried to harm you would be too stunned to say anything in return.

How is New York? Is there snow? I haven't seen snow in the longest time. Not since before the Dust Bowl, anyway. I pine for it.

Your little sister,
Bess Rowland

P.S. Thank you for the note with your address.

January 10th, 1936

Dear Bess,

I tried not to let my emotions get the best of me when I received your letter. I opened it with a stiff upper lip and would not allow myself to feel anything but cheerful as I read it. But it didn't work. I felt ... I felt a smorgasbord (isn't that a funny word?) of emotions. First, I felt angry. Papa just doesn't understand me, and I don't understand him. I know I did the right thing, coming to New York like I did. Why can't he see that? But then I felt wishy-washy when I thought of Mama, Donny, and you. Finally, I felt like a rebel and an adventurer, striking out on my own in this lively city.

Thank you for not being cross. But I wish you could understand why I left. You know, as well as I, that the farm isn't doing well. Papa doesn't dare talk about it in front of you and Donny. Doesn't want you to worry. We're poor, Bess. We're just hanging on. New York City must have a job for me. Then I can send money home. Papa doesn't like the idea of his twenty-year-old girl bringing home the dough, but the other option is starving. Which would you prefer?

My heart was restless, Bess. I dearly love our farm and the wide plains of Kansas, but after looking at them for twenty years, I needed to see something else. You know I've always been adventure stricken. I smile as I think of the pictures of far off places plastered to our bedroom wall. Are they still there, or did you pull them down? Did you see the one of New York City bathed in morning sunlight? That's what I'm seeing from my window, finally.

The train ride was smashing. I snuggled into the corner of my seat, leaned my face against the cold window and watched as Missouri, Illinois, Indiana, Ohio, Pennsylvania, and New Jersey whizzed past. See? Just taking a trip to New York allows me to see six states I wouldn't have had the chance to see. It was a long trip, but I passed the time by reading, dreaming, and sketching. I'll show you the sketchings of scenery and people I met along the way next time I see you. One woman was an opera singer, one man was a magician. It's fascinating, the people you meet while traveling.

Once I arrived in the dear, lively city, I needed a place to live—something I hadn't had the wits to think about before. But that didn't prove to be a problem after all. I found a sweet little boarding house run by a middle aged woman who likes to wear polka dots.

I was exhausted from the trip, so I quickly slipped into my pajamas and fell into the bed near the window. City lights danced on the walls, and I could hear the constant refrain of honking and pedestrians' voices. It took a long while before I could drift to sleep. It's so different than falling asleep to the sounds of nature at home. I suppose it will take me a spell to adjust.

Tomorrow starts my job hunt. The possibilities are endless here! Who knows ... your older sister might just become a famous actress, or maybe a world-renowned journalist. Can't you see my name in lights —*Georgiana Rowland*. It'll be great news for the people back home when they read: *Kansas Girl Takes New York City!* Wish me well! Keep me updated on homelife. I miss you, Bess. You're the only one whom I can confide in.

Your sister,

Georgiana

P.S. Yes, there's snow. A heap of it! Wish I could send you some.

January 19th, 1936

Gi,

This depression our country has fallen in is just that: *depressing*. Isn't it interesting how the government appropriately names economic disasters?

What I mean is that Papa is looking rather crestfallen. No, that's not the word for it. Dejected. Downtrodden. Depressed. Like I said, the government knows what it's talking about. The fact that you have left is only adding to the crestfallen feeling. Even our little old house is looking sad. The eaves seem to droop a little more, and the paint is looking a bit more chipped and careworn. I noticed this because I climbed over the fence to the empty, ugly house across the street and stared at our porch for awhile. It was prettier before the Dust Bowl hit.

All this observation happened, you see, because I was supposed to be sweeping the porch of that empty, ugly house across the street. Old Mr. Thomas is supposedly coming back to live there. I don't remember him much, but I suppose you do. All I know of him is that after he heard that his daughter and son-in-law died, he up and left without so much as a goodbye. He's coming back now. I wonder if the depression took its toll on him too and left him nothing but this wisp of a house. It's bigger than ours, for sure. But it's a bit more careworn, it seems. It looks as if it's seen a tragedy. I wonder if it has?

Mrs. Yale gathered several ladies from church and had us spruce it up. That's why I was standing on the porch of the house across the street. That's why I observed the depression of our dear little home.

I must say, I was rather disappointed in you, Georgiana Rowland. I have not taken down your pictures, thank you very much. I kept them up because they remind me of you. I know the one of New York very well. But my favorite is the one of our beloved Kansas prairies. They're bathed in sunlight and whisper the word "home" to me. The same way the stark brown dust whispers the word "home" beneath my feet.

Why did they not whisper the same words to you?

All that to say, I'll keep you updated on home, but there's not much to say about it. It's much the same as when you left. Except you aren't here, and Mama (still) cries every night. I'm considering just moving Donny's bed into our—my—room.

Goodnight, Gi. It's late. Mama and Papa have shut themselves in their room, and I suspect the tears will start again soon. Donny will stumble into my room and tell me a story.

Sleep well.

Bess

January 25th, 1936

Dear Bess,

Oh, Papa. Isn't he always dejected? I mean no disrespect, but he's always worrying. I can't stand it! Why can't he just *live*? If only he could see New York … he'd certainly take on another attitude! The problem with Papa is that he's never traveled. He's been stuck on that farm in the middle of no man's land since the day he was born. I doubt I'll ever come back to Kansas for good. New York has spoiled me, I suppose.

Old Mr. Thomas is coming back? How will he survive with times being so hard in Kansas, and no one to care for him? But I'm sure you'll help him out, won't you, Bess? And send Donny over to tell him stories.

I have to say, I'm having a great time during this Great Depression. Is that horrible for me to say? Well, I just said it. New York is grand, Bess! This is the life I've always dreamed of! I woke up to the sun shining in through my window, promising a lovely day. I immediately scampered to the window and pulled open the curtains. I smiled as my eyes met a city alive! Huge buildings rose through the morning fog, vendors were situated on their corners, and couples laughed, arms linked, as they strolled down the street. *Sigh.* It's lovely.

Well, then I dressed and tried to do something with my wild hair (it isn't easy) and hurried downstairs. The landlady—Mrs. West—gave me toast with strawberry jam and a cold glass of milk. Small portions, of course, but delicious nonetheless. I was introduced to the other boarders. There's a young couple who are musicians. They both play the violin … or was it the viola? Then there's a mother and her ten-year-old son, both looking for work. The boy, Karl, knocked over my coffee this morning and stained my best skirt. Little devil. Then there's a young journalist, Mr. Willoughby Reeves. Dashing fellow with nice eyes. But his name—*Willoughby?* Poor lad.

I looked for a job … briefly. It was my first day in the dear old city, so I allowed myself to take it all in. I took a trolley, fed a few birds, then found a restaurant and paid 15 cents for a sandwich and orange juice. I desperately want to see a Broadway show. Perhaps I will one of these days.

Tomorrow I'm looking for a job in earnest. But I won't settle for washing dishes or something horrible like that. I'm in New York for heaven's sake! I have the world at my fingertips.

– Gi

February 1st, 1936

Dear Gi,

I've never traveled, and I feel quite content here on the farm. I mean no offense to you, of course, but I believe that my cases of wanderlust are quite different from yours. I don't quite understand them. Sometimes I want to run, run, run. Other times, I can't bear the thought of running.

Speaking of running, I ran again the other night. Donny had nodded off to sleep after telling his story to me. Mama's sobbing had ceased, and Papa's snores had started. I slipped out of my bed, caught a glimpse of the stars through the window, and tip-toed downstairs. The creaky door never creaks on these nights. It's almost like magic.

It was cool and misty out-of-doors. The winter air kills me these days, but the nights are far too eerie for me to evade the cold. My breath caught in my throat when I looked up at the stars. They are fascinating, Gi. I wish I was a star. Almost.

I flopped onto the hay bale in the wire-fenced field and crossed my arms over my chest. It was a wanderlust night. The stars spoke to my soul, and I sprang off the hay bale. The cold, dry grass stung my feet as I tore through that field, and for once, I didn't mind the pain.

I was nearing the edge of the fence by the scraggly trees and the mud hole (what used to be known as the swimming hole, if you recall). Of a sudden, I tripped over something and went tumbling to the ground. I gasped and wiped my knees before turning to see what I had tripped on.

Gi, it was a body.

I had a perfect heart attack right then. I'd never had a heart attack before. It was a peculiar feeling. I screeched out loud and recoiled, ready to run and tell Papa there had been a murder when the body spoke to me. It wasn't a body at all, Gi. Well, of course it was, but there was a living boy in it. He turned his head calmly toward me and said, "Hello."

That was all. I said "hello" back.

He sat up, scrubbing his hands through his tousled hair and said, "I'm Tom."

I was rather speechless. I tend to be rather speechless when I meet young men whom I assumed dead in my field at midnight.

I'm pretty certain Tom and I stared at one another for a full two minutes before I did anything. I stretched out my hand and said, "Hello." Again. Then I said, "Who are you?"

"Tom." The boy looked pretty amused. "I'm Mr. Thomas' grandson."

Did you know old Mr. Thomas had a grandson, Gi? I didn't. Mama says she didn't either. I don't think anyone did. Yesterday they came to church, and Mr. Thomas got lots of startled looks from the congregation. Even Reverend Wilkins looked his way nine times during his sermon. I counted.

"If your last name is Thomas," I said in confusion. "Why is your first name Tom?"

Tom looked at me and said, "My last name is James, ma'am. My mother was the daughter of Mr. Thomas. I was named after him. Do you understand?"

He was teasing me there. He was taunting my ignorance. I just knew it. However, I handled it with dignity. I said, "That's stupid."

Tom agreed. He said I could call him Jimmy if I wanted to. I declined because Tom sounds nicer than Jimmy. Wouldn't you agree?

And that's the news I have for you from Kansas. There's a ginger living across the road from me. Did I mention Tom is a ginger? Rumors say he graduated from a very high-class private school in New York. Not New York City, but somewhere in New York. I don't know where they got that idea because I stumbled across Tom on Saturday night; Mr. Thomas and Tom came to church Sunday morning and left without speaking to anyone (though I suspected Tom wanted to). And it is now Monday, and no one has seen hide nor hair of them since.

Oh, Donny says to tell you that we ran out of pickled beets today. He is most upset.

I'm worried as well, Gi. Not about the pickled beets but because the cellar is so empty of much food. Ever since that stupid dust bowl, you know how ill our crops have been. The other day I went to pick up some flour from the store for Mama. I saw Mr. Yale write it down on our tab, and do you know that we are fifty-two dollars in debt to him? Fifty-two dollars, Gi!

I still don't understand you. But I'm beginning to understand what you did.

Much love,
     Bess

February 12th, 1936

My dear Bess,

My goodness, you tripped over a boy? How queer. I didn't know that Mr. Thomas had a grandson, but he sounds like a charming lad. And ginger headed … how fortunate for him. Ginger is a nice color. Do Mama and Papa know that you were running outside in the middle of the night? Not that I would tell them. It just seems rather adventurous of you. Bravo my dear! But do be careful. There are hobos on the loose, you know.

I looked for a job today. I dressed in my most professional looking attire—the floral patterned dress with lace around the collar—wore my locket and those hand-me-down heels from Aunt Diana, though they were rather scuffed. I was going to put my hair up, but those stubborn curls kept springing into my eyes. So I wore it down instead, topped with my gray hat situated at a becoming angle. Mama wouldn't like it, but I wore bright red lipstick. Ah, look at me, Bess! Aren't I a rebel?

I took a trolley (because it's so classy) into the heart of the city. I read about auditions for a musical earlier this morning. It wasn't a Broadway musical, but one has to start somewhere. My goodness! The line was atrocious! I stood there in the bitter cold, hopping from one heel to the other in a desperate attempt to keep warm. I would have grabbed a cup of coffee, but I didn't dare get out of line. A few hours passed, and it was finally my turn. The auditorium was packed full of people. The stage was as big as our barn back home. Ornate carvings adorned the walls, and the chairs were red velvet. It was rather dark and stuffy in there, but I was too excited to care much.

Bess, I was so silly. I didn't even know exactly what I was trying out for. Apparently it involved a lot of tap dancing. You know that I can't dance to save my life. They gave me a pair of tap shoes for the audition. There I stood in the middle of a stage that swallowed me up and made me feel like a little bug.

"Dance," they said.

I don't know what a shuffle or a back brush step is, so I winged it. But I didn't wing it well enough. Oh, Bess! I completely embarrassed myself and nearly fell off the stage! My face is red just thinking about it! I ripped those shoes off my feet and left that place, feeling like I needed some coffee. So that's what I did. I drank five cups of coffee and then felt like running around Central Park fifty times. Remind me to limit my caffeine intake and to never audition for a tap dance routine.

Don't worry, Bess. I know fifty-two dollars in debt is a bunch, but I did get a part time job. It doesn't pay much, but I'm a seamstress for a small sewing shop down the road. Mrs. West and I also made a deal. I'll dust and clean the boarding house in exchange for free meals.

I wonder what tomorrow will bring. You just never know in this darling city.

Hugs!

Gi

February 16th, 1936

Dearest Gi,

I fell off the church roof this morning. In fact, it was only a few hours ago. I fled the scene of the crime. I am mortified. I am never leaving our—my—bedroom again.

I slept in this morning. It was entirely on accident. I was up late reading by moonlight last night. Normally not waking up in time wouldn't be a bother because Mama would have woken me up. But I'd told her the day before that I was intending on leaving for church much earlier than they. I had been recruited to help set up for the church social taking place in the afternoon.

Well, needless to say, I was late for church.

I rolled over in my bed a couple times, blinked my eyes, and suddenly sat up in a wild fit. It was light outside! The sun was up! My church dress hung limply from my closet door! I was dreadfully late. I felt much like the Rabbit from *Alice in Wonderland*. I glanced at the clock. It read 10:47. Church started at

10:30. I sprang from my bed, scrambled into my dress, and ran downstairs. I slid down the banister. It seemed like the fastest option at the moment, but trust me, Gi, when I say it was a stupid idea. My dress caught and tore. A great gash down the side. It didn't tear too far as to be indecent so I just shed a couple tears and ran out the door. I forgot my shoes. The ground was dusty and very cold. And I had forgotten my coat.

I was miserable at this point and already embarrassed.

I ran down the road, tying my hair up with a ribbon as I went. This proved another terrible idea. As I neared the church and struggled to wrap the ribbon around my hair with cold, stiff fingers, a wind gushed through and stole the ribbon from my hands. It went sailing through the air, and do you know where it landed? It wrapped lightly around the church spire and caught there.

I think I spat out some incoherent exclamations and stomped around in the dust for a moment. I looked at the great wooden door to the church. It was shut. I could hear Reverend Wilkins' voice booming inside. I bit my lip until I tasted blood and then remembered the old ladder behind the church. It was heavy, but after many tries I managed to lean it against the back porch. And then I climbed up to the church roof.

Do you understand how absolutely frightening it is to climb on a church roof during a gusty winter day? I doubt you would. You'd probably claim it was "exhilarating" or something of the sort. I don't understand you, Gi.

I didn't think through my actions. You probably could have pointed that out by now. After all, how on earth was I going to climb up that slender church spire? Well. I wrapped my arms and legs around it and tried scooting up. It didn't work at all. Besides, the skirt to my sad, torn dress kept getting in the way.

After several attempts, I was thoroughly cold, and I realized that going into church with tangled hair was better than fetching a hair ribbon from the church spire. It must have been 11:00 by then anyway, and the sermon would likely be over within an hour. I wasn't sparing myself any time or embarrassment standing there on the roof.

So I inched my way back to the ladder.

That's when a particularly strong gust of wind burst through. I wobbled on that roof, Gi. I think my life flashed before my eyes in that instant. It was quite, quite scary. I didn't fall, however. But something else did.

I heard a crash below me, and my breath caught in my throat. I scrambled quickly toward the ladder—or where the ladder should have been. There I was, crouched on that porch roof looking down at that ladder that had fallen and lain flat on the ground.

I was doomed. I knew it. Either I was to embarrass myself and catch a cold by waiting for the sermon to finish, so I could holler for Papa's help. Or I could attempt to squirm down the roof supports and walk into the church with a few scattered pieces of dignity still stuck to me. I chose the latter. Stupid, stupid Bess.

I'm sure you understand that I fell. Not completely, but I fell partway. My life flashed before my eyes again, and then my arms wrenched as I caught the gutter. I hung there. Like a sack of cornmeal. And good Lord, did I scream. I screamed pretty loudly. And the next thing I knew, the back door of the church was flung open, and the entire congregation poured out. I think they all sort of paused in shock. I hung there with tangled hair, a torn dress, and terror written across my face. The next thing I knew, Papa and Reverend Wilkins had run and got the ladder. Papa climbed up and grabbed me by the waist. I finally stood on solid ground again. I turned around and faced the congregation.

With the panic gone, Gi, I suddenly drowned in embarrassment. It was the most awful thing I've ever experienced. I think I stuttered the word "hair ribbon" and then high-tailed it back home.

It's 3:04 now. Everyone's enjoying the church social at this moment, I guess. I'll probably get a tongue-lashing when Mama and Papa and Donny get home. Then I will reveal the fact that I'm never leaving my room again. Ever. Then I will ... *Good gracious.*

9:54 P.M.

That was Tom. I mean, the interruption was caused by Tom. What I mean to say is it was a long interruption, I agree. And I'm still never going to leave my room again. At least, not for a very long time.

Tom was staring at me through the bedroom window! It's scandalous, Gi. He climbed all the way up the porch roof. With my hair ribbon! He was grinning at me through the window, my red hair ribbon hidden in his fist.

"Hey," he said. "You never told me your name when we met in the field."

"I didn't?" I asked, quite taken aback that a ginger had been staring at me through my bedroom window for who knows how long. Thank heavens I was only writing a letter.

"No," Tom told me and laughed.

"Oh!" I said, realizing I'd not yet told him my name. "I'm Bess. Bess Rowland."

"Bess." He grinned. That's when he gave me the hair ribbon. My cheeks turned so hot, Gi. He probably saw the whole scene.

"Thanks," I stammered and refused to look him in the eye.

"Hey," Tom said again, leaning on my window sill. "Whatcha writing?"

"A letter to my sister," I replied, covering the pages with my arms. "She's away in New York City."

"Really?" Tom went on to tell me how he's been to New York and went to school in Albany. He's seventeen, too, Gi. But he's so boyish I would have guessed he was fifteen.

All that to say, Tom convinced me to come to the church social. I'm not sure how he did it, but he's very clever, and when I refused at first, he had such a boyish, wheedling way of begging me to come, I couldn't say no.

That's why I'm not leaving my room again for a very long time. Someone brought a fiddle to the church social, and Tom suddenly swung me into a reckless dance. It was fun until I twisted my ankle. I tried not to show it, but I was in a lot of pain. Papa had to carry me home. It's turning purple and blue now. Mama had the doctor come, and he said I can't walk on it for three or four weeks.

But funny enough, I'm not terribly upset about it. Tom said he'll come over as often as he can to visit me. He feels pretty awful about it all. But the point is, I've made a friend. I've never had a friend before besides you, Gi.

The original intent in sharing all of this was to gain sympathy and show you that your audition incident wasn't as embarrassing as falling off the church roof. But now I think I'll just say that you never know what might come of embarrassing situations. I made a friend who cares about my ankles and my hair ribbons.

And I've gotten out of chores for three weeks.

Your bedridden sister,

Bess

February 21st, 1936

Oh Bess!

What a tragical (in the words of Miss Anne Shirley) ordeal you went through! I wish I could have seen the looks on everyone's faces as you dangled from the roof! What a laugh! Me-oh-my, that Tom fellow is rather forward. It sounds like he's taken quite a fancy to my sweet little sister, Bess. How darling! Tell me more stories about him. I like that boy, and I haven't even met him. He sounds the opposite of you, which I think works nicely.

Well, sis, you're going to be rather cross and astonished at me. I tried to sneak into a Broadway show today. Without paying. It was all Karl's fault, the horrible snotty-nosed boy. He lured me into it. Here's how it went:

I was sighing over not being able to afford a ticket to see a Broadway show last evening. I sat in the parlor, feet up on a stool and pouring over my movie star magazines—the ones Mama and Papa call "frivolous." Karl's mother had just left the room to fetch tea. The boy inched toward me, his brown eyes bright.

"I know how to get into a Broadway show for free."

I set down my magazine. "And how would you know that?"

"Do it all the time."

It piqued my interest, Bess. You know how much I've always longed to see a Broadway show! So I said, "Do elaborate."

He sat on the arm of the sofa. "You don't get to see the whole show, but it's still swell. You go in at intermission when all the muckety-mucks are talkin' and smokin' their cigars. We join the group. But we can't wear our coats … that'd give it away that we came in off the streets."

"But what about seats? If we just sat wherever we pleased, a ticket holder would have us thrown out in an instant. See? Your plan is flawed."

He shook his head. "Let me finish, lady! All the ticket holders' seats are down when they leave. We just have to find seats that are up. Got it? And you gotta act confident. If you look nervous, they'll be on to you."

The little devil was ingenious. And tricky. "Why you little stinker," was all I said.

He gave me a lopsided grin. "So, want to come? I could pretend that I'm your little brother. Looks better than me sneakin' in with my buddies all the time."

And Bess, against my better judgment I said yes. Then I heard footsteps in the hallway and felt a chill run up my spine. Suppose one of the other boarders heard about our rebellious scheme? But no one came in, and I breathed normally again.

That evening found Karl and I ditching our jackets in a phone booth. We hurriedly stormed into the theater, and I followed Karl, imitating his calm, know-it-all attitude. Puffs of cigar smoke stung my eyes, and I couldn't see where I was going. I bumped into someone. Someone I sorta know. Willoughby Reeves, that dashing journalist.

"Oh dear!" I yelped.

"Good evening, Miss Rowland," he said, then glanced down at Karl. "Karl," he nodded his head toward the youngster.

"Evening good to me, too," I said. *I said that.* Oh, when will I stop embarrassing myself, Bess? I was so nervous that I couldn't speak a simple sentence! I felt as if the police would come from every corner, encircle me, and then drag me off to jail. Maybe they'd torture me—hang me up by my thumbs!

I dared a glance at Mr. Reeves. His head was down, but I saw a smirk overtake his handsome face. Did I just write *handsome*? Oh dear. Too bad this is in ink, otherwise I'd have erased that.

"So, are you two enjoying the show? What do you think of the first half?"

My limbs felt like jello. "Uh … " I looked for Karl, hoping he'd help me out of this, but the little rat was gone! "It was lovely! So very beautiful!" I said, rubbing my sweaty palms together.

Mr. Reeves raised a brow. "Oh? That's interesting that you think so, considering half of the characters died in the first half. But if you like that sorta thing … "

"Did you think I said *lovely*? I said … *bloody*. It was bloody. And … and so very *rueful*."

I'm so uncreative under pressure, Bess.

Again that man smirked! "I see," he said. "Who's your favorite character so far?"

I dearly wished I hadn't let that boy talk me into sneaking into this show. What was I to do now? My mind was drained of any ideas to save me from this dreadful talk. I recalled your last letter and blurted out: "Tom. He's a great guy."

This time, Mr. Reeves burst out laughing. At me! Of all the humiliating things! But I thought I could still save myself. "What? Isn't that his name?"

"No guy named Tom is in this play, Miss Rowland. Perhaps you got his name wrong? Or perhaps Karl talked you into the classic game kids do for fun in New York—sneaking into Broadway shows?"

I was floored. "Mr. Reeves—"

"Will," he said. "Call me Will."

"Mr. Reeves ... " (I wasn't about to call him Will after he accused me and all.) "You think so poorly of me as to jump to the conclusion that I sneaked in without paying?"

"I don't think poorly of you, Miss Rowland. But yes, I do believe you sneaked in here."

Good grief. I wish he'd wipe that charming grin off his charming face. And then all at once I found myself confessing. "You're right, actually. Good job." What? I was congratulating him for finding me out? What a dunce I am! Then I curtsied and wished him a goodnight. But he grabbed my elbow as I was turning.

"Aren't you going to stay and watch the second half?"

"No, I'm not. You've made me feel guilty for sneaking in."

"I'll pay for you."

Oh, Bess. I wanted to say yes. I desperately did. But I'm not a charity case, and so I simply said, "No, thank you. I should get back to the boarding house."

"Then I'll walk you home," he said.

"No, that's not necessary. Wouldn't want you to miss seeing who dies next in this charming show." Then I slipped through the crowd before he could say anything else. I didn't know where Karl went ... figured he must already be comfortably seated and eager to watch the show. Isn't that nice for him? *Groan.*

I retrieved my jacket from the phone booth and hoofed it through the busy streets, keeping my head bent low. It was so dark, but I was too embarrassed by that little chat with Reeves to be afraid of walking alone at night in the city. I made it back to the boarding house (safe and sound) and asked Mrs. West if I could make a cup of tea. I took it up to my room and gulped it down, hoping I wouldn't run into Reeves *ever* again.

Well, what do you think of your older sister? Are you ashamed? Please, don't be. I've learned my lesson.

Until next time,

Gi

February 26th, 1936

Georgiana,

If you don't mind my saying so, I think your handsome Mr. Reeves has taken quite a fancy to you.

And I am awfully cross at you for suggesting such a thing about Tom. I was quite alright with just being good friends with him. I thought he was merely being friendly with me. Stop putting such ideas in my head, Georgiana Rowland. I may be seventeen, but I think I'm still a child. Aren't I? Sometimes I doubt it, Gi. And that scares me. Mama got married when she was eighteen. Do you think that might happen to me? I rather hope not, but one can't be sure.

On that note, I will relay to you the events that have taken place since I last wrote you. You recall that I twisted my ankle while dancing with Tom, don't you? Well, I suppose you also remember how I said I was afraid I would catch a cold standing on top of the church in such wretched temperatures. I did. I was bedridden with a miserable cold for nearly two weeks.

I'm still bedridden now with that swollen ankle of mine.

And then our electricity got turned off. Papa couldn't pay the electric bill. I don't like to be a thorn in the side, but do tell me if you have yet gotten a well-paying job, Gi? I can't help but worry. I've moved downstairs by the fireside because my room is chilly now. Donny sleeps on blankets by the hearth, and I've been on the sofa for four days.

It's better for socializing, anyway.

Tom seems to assume that I am having the most dreadful time being stuck on the sofa, but to be truthful, I don't really mind. There's not much to see out of doors these days anyway. There's dust. Dry grass. And winter air. The only thing I miss is the stars at night. I can hardly see them through the window.

I read a lot these days. Donny dug under your bed to find some of your old books for me, and he found your dog-eared copy of *Little Women*. Do you know that I think it's my favorite book now? I've just reached the part where Laurie fools with Meg's emotions by sending her a prank love letter from John. Isn't that just too mean?

As you can see, there hasn't been much happening around here besides losing our electricity. I read. I sleep. I think. I talk to Mama and Donny. Oh, and I talk with Tom, too. I think it's fair to say we are quite good friends now. His shenanigans (isn't that a fun word?) amuse me so. And just guess what he did yesterday! (I've been saving this bit of best news for last.) He brought me a kitten! It's a dear, darling thing, Gi! You would love it. I named her Priss because she's a prissy little kitty. She's a tabby with the most exquisite little whiskers and paws. She sleeps at the foot of my bed—sofa, I mean. Tom says she's a lion to guard me at night. Not sure where he got that idea since she's just a wee bit bigger than a mouse.

Anyway, please tell me about all your recent adventures. I've been imagining the most beautiful stories in my head about you and—you'll murder me for this—Mr. Reeves. I'm sorry. I just can't help it. I have too much time on my hands.

I miss you.

    Bess

P.S. I made a discovery the other day. Tom is Laurie!

March 2nd, 1936

Dear Bess,

Well! Aren't you getting cheeky, Miss Elisabeth Ann Rowland, suggesting that Mr. Reeves has taken a fancy to me. If I was home, I'd have thrown a pillow at you for that. And I have good aim.

I still think you and Tom are adorable. You will send me a photograph of you two, won't you? Poor dear, being bedridden. I'm so glad you found my copy of *Little Women*. I get a warm, fuzzy feeling just thinking about that story!

The electricity was turned off?! Oh, that's horrible, Bess! I would send you money right away but—I kinda blew it today with the whole job thing. It's my pride flaring up, Bess! I can't seem to tame it!

You know how I wished I'd never see Willoughby Reeves again? I did. God sure has a sense of humor, throwing me back into Mr. Reeves' presence after that criminal Broadway ordeal and my last bit of complete humiliation. You recall that I wrote about his handsome face in my last letter? Well, I was sitting in the parlor when I was writing it. I got up quickly because Mrs. West needed help carrying something into the kitchen, and I abandoned my letter, thinking no one would read it. When I entered the parlor once more, my insides twisted. Karl had my letter in his hands ... and he was showing it to *Willoughby Reeves*. My face burned horribly as Reeves turned to glance at me. He had read it, all right, for he smiled and said, "I have a handsome face, Miss Rowland? Glad to hear that."

Ugh! I could have slugged Karl, but that wouldn't have been very ladylike, would it? Instead, I fled to my room. I tried avoiding Mr. Reeves. He always eats early at the boarding house, so I ate once he had left the table. I hadn't run into him—until today.

I had spent the morning job hunting and retired to a quaint little coffee shop to rest for a while. (I thought you were going to remind me to limit my caffeine intake?) I had polished off nine cups of joe when that man entered the coffee shop. I saw him before he saw me, so I shrank down in my seat and looked down at my hands. When I glanced up, there he was, taking the seat across from me like he owned the place.

"Good morning, Mr. Reeves," I said. "What are you doing here?"

"Good morning," he said. "I thought I told you to call me Will, Miss Rowland."

Miss Rowland was starting to sound like I was a strict teacher, so I nipped that name in the bud. "My name's Georgiana, but everyone calls me Gi."

"Gi. I like it."

I blushed but quickly regained my composure. "You didn't answer my question, Mr ... I mean ... Will. What are you doing here?" I wasn't yet accustomed to calling him such a casual name as that.

"Getting coffee. What about you, Gi?"

"Same."

A few seconds of awkward silence. I fidgeted in my chair.

"See any Broadway shows recently?" he asked.

Of all the things to ask me! "No."

"Get a full time job yet?"

"No."

"Have enough money to pay rent?"

I glanced up at him. "Of course." I hadn't calculated yet, but I was sure I wasn't broke. Not yet anyway.

"Good. I'm glad to hear that." He took a sip of coffee.

My cup was completely empty. Only stains in the white porcelain proved I'd been drinking any.

"Want more coffee?" Willoughby asked.

I pushed my cup toward him. "Please."

Well, that was a bad idea. Ten cups of coffee in my system is *never* a good thing.

"Are you all right?" Willoughby asked as I tapped my fingers on the table in record speed.

"Feeling like I need to walk," I said. "I have a weakness for coffee. Ten cups has put me over the edge."

His brown eyes widened, and a smirk tugged on his lips. "*Ten* cups?"

I nodded.

"I'd like to write an article on you."

"Me?"

"What ten cups of coffee can do to a person. I think it'd be interesting."

I rolled my eyes. "I need to go … run a marathon." I pushed away from the table and hurried out the coffee shop. Willoughby was on my heels.

"Can I run a marathon with you? I have something to ask you."

"I'm not going to be the subject of an article, Will."

EMILY CHAPMAN & EMILY ANN PUTZKE

"No, no, no. I was jesting about that, Gi. I was wondering if you needed help finding a job."

I quickened my pace to a jog. Oh, caffeine was running through my blood at a furious speed. I blame what happens next on that.

"Me? Need help? I can find a job on my own, thank you very much." My insides were all jumbled together. My heels click-clacked on the sidewalk as I pushed through a throng of people.

"Are you sure?" he said, jogging next to me. "I could get you one."

"I can find a job, Will. Believe me. I know what I'm doing." I should have humbled myself and at least listened to his idea, but I didn't. I guess I wanted to prove to him, and to everyone, that I am independent. I'm sorry, Bess. I *will* get a real job. I promise.

If there's one thing I've learned since moving to NYC, it's this: I'll never type in permanent ink that Willoughby Reeves is handsome ever again. Oh! *Blast!* Bess, I did it again! I don't see the likes of Karl anywhere ... I'll send this right away, so he doesn't get his grubby fingers on it. Oh, the humiliation!

How are Mama and Papa faring? Is Papa still stubborn as ever?

– Gi

March 9th, 1936

Dearest sister of mine,

I am pleased to say that my ankle is finally better.

Before I tell you the tale of how Donny and I almost spent the night alone on the wintery Kansas prairies, let me say that you ought to swallow your pride and ask Will (may I call him Will too?) for that job. You're a fool, Georgiana Reeves—gracious, did I just say Georgiana *Reeves*? I can't help it if I've been calling you that in my head for two weeks. I'm sorry, Gi. I must say, in this particular moment, I am very glad you are far away in New York City. Your aim is impeccable, and I just recovered from an injury.

Now, this is how Donny and I almost spent the entire night on the prairie. Oh, and Tom was there, too.

I was finally walking around a bit and feeling the ache of being cooped up in the house. I was sitting on the front porch, my feet dangling over the edge, when that wild urge of wanderlust crossed me again. I hadn't felt that urge in a long, long time. I kicked my heels against the side of the porch and decided I needed to run somewhere. It was a much warmer day than it had been for weeks—sixty-two degrees out, the thermometer read.

"Donny!" I called, and his little face appeared at the screen door. There were splotches of flour on his chubby cheeks. He had been helping Mama bake our little loaves of bread. (I say little because they've been getting littler and littler lately.) "Do you want to go explore with me?"

"Will it be dangerous?" he asked me, his big brown eyes wide.

I didn't want to lie to him, Gi, so I told him, "It might be." Chills ran down my legs when I thought of it. I remembered you telling me to be careful because there were hobos on the loose. "There might be hobos," I gravely told Donny.

"What's a hobo?" he asked me, opening the creaky screen door and plopping down next to me.

"It's a homeless person," I said, pulling my knees up to my chest. "Gi said they're dangerous."

"Oh." Donny propped his chin up with his fists for a moment before saying, "C'mon, Bess."

So we went exploring. We were only a few feet down the road when a screen door slammed, and we heard Tom shouting, "Where are you headed?"

I turned and found him barreling toward us. "We're going exploring," I told him, rather glad he was coming along. I was still a little frightened about the hobos. "Want to come?"

He did, of course. So the three of us walked for quite a long time. We walked down our road, but the opposite way. We didn't walk toward town. We walked toward the open prairie instead. I'd been down that way before, but I hadn't been down there as far as we walked. Poor Donny got really tired, so Tom swung him up on his shoulders. Once Tom asked me if I wanted to go back, and I don't know what possessed me to say, "No. Let's leave the road and see where the land takes us."

Unfortunately, Tom didn't seem the slightest bit doubtful. If he had, I would have gone back. But he didn't. He laughed and said, "Okay." And charged straight into the dry prairie grasses.

You're probably beginning to understand why we almost spent the night out-of-doors. We got lost. Very lost. You see, eventually I said, "Let's go back now." The sun was beginning to lower pretty violently, and I realized we would be late for supper.

Tom agreed we should head back. Then he looked at me, scratched his head, turned around several times and said, "Which way is back?"

That's when we both realized we were lost. Donny started to cry. I sat down in the middle of the grass, buried my face in my knees, and contemplated why I was so stupid. Apparently these actions made Tom very uncomfortable, for he sat down next to me, took Donny on his knee, and patted my shoulder saying, "C'mon, Bess, it's not so bad. We just have to find our way back. We walked here well enough. Surely we can walk back."

Wasn't that nice of him? I think he sent a surge of bravery through me, for I lifted my head suddenly and patted Donny's back, saying, "Tom's right, Donny-boy."

Tom grinned at me, stood up with Donny balanced in his arms, and held his hand out saying, "Let's go traverse back home, mademoiselle."

He's so cocky, Gi.

So you see, we attempted to find our way back home. Eventually the sunset glimmered before our eyes, and we realized it was getting awfully close to dinnertime. Then the sun set, and we realized it was dinnertime. And we were definitely missing it. Then Donny grew so tired he fell asleep with his head bobbing on Tom's shoulder, and the stars began to come out. That was the highlight of the evening, Gi. I hadn't seen the stars on open prairie before. I stopped in my tracks when multitudes of them came peeping out, and Tom turned to look at me. "Say," he said, "let's stargaze."

"What do you mean?" I asked, rather mesmerized by the stars and only half hearing what he said.

"That's what I was doing when you tripped over me," he explained, gently laying Donny down in the grass. The poor fellow didn't stir once.

I blinked as Tom lay down next to him. Then I let the sharp grasses envelop me, and I stared at the stars. They were beautiful. Surges of wanderlust shot through me, and my heart swelled. I love the stars. I never feel myself around them. I can't really explain it. But it's beautiful.

"The moon is distant from the sea," Tom suddenly murmured. "And yet with amber hands she leads him, docile as a boy, along appointed sands."

I sat up in surprise. "Does the moon make you feel like that?"

Tom sat up, leaning his arms on his knees. "That was Emily Dickinson," he said.

"Yes, I know," I said impatiently, waving my hands. "But the moon. Does it make you feel like … like wanderlust. Or like the wind that foreshadows a rainstorm? Or … or like a ship broken from shore and bobbing on the wide, open ocean. Or perhaps like a bird flying above an endless wood where—"

Tom caught my arm, chuckling. "Don't hurt yourself," he said, and I felt very disappointed as I lay back down, gazing at the stars above me.

"No," I heard him murmur, "it makes me feel more like … more like a prisoner just set free."

I think I cried then, Gi.

"Does the moon make you feel that way, too?" Tom asked me.

"No," I said, smiling. "The stars."

We lay there for a long time, staring at the heavens. Then Donny stirred and said, "Where's Mama?" And we realized we ought to find our way back home.

We never found our way back home. Papa and old Mr. Thomas found us. When we didn't come home for dinner, Mama had sent them out to look for us. Papa's a genius when it comes to finding things. Remember how he found our little milk cow when we looked and looked all day and couldn't find her? And remember how he found our sled buried beneath that pile of snow? Yes, I think Papa should become a professional finder. They had taken the truck out and started combing the prairie for us. And they found us. Tom and I rode in the back on the way home. It was bumpy over the prairie, and it lulled me to sleep. I woke up to find my head resting on Tom's shoulder. It was embarrassing.

When we got home, Priss mewed and rubbed her little self around my legs. "Tom said she was supposed to be a lion to guard me at night," I laughed, stroking her as Mama picked up our sleepy Donny to bring him to bed. "She didn't do a very good job of it tonight!"

"She didn't need to," Donny piped up. "Tom was there."

I went to get something to eat with Priss on my heels.

And there you have my first big adventure story. It was a fascinating day, Gi. But I don't think I would want to become a regular adventurer.

Now that you have finished reading this, please go talk to Will and ask him for that job.

Your sister,

Bess

P.S. Tone down on the caffeine intake, my dear.

March 15th, 1936

Bess!

Georgiana *Reeves*?! Really, must you tease me like this? Although, it does look rather nice, doesn't it ... *Oh!* You've lured me into your scheme, you little stinker! And I can't ask Will for that job now. Not after I snapped at him while having a "ten cups of coffee" panic attack! You just don't understand. Don't take up coffee drinking, Bess. You'll never stop ... and you probably won't get a job.

I must say, your little adventure in the Kansas prairie sounds exhilarating! Oh, I almost wish I could have been there. How lovely it must have been to look up at a sky peppered with stars. I haven't seen many stars since coming here. The city lights drown them out.

Now, Bess, about Tom ... It's obvious to everyone (I'm sure) but *yourself* that he's smitten with you. Can't you see? Oh, of course you can't. Just mark my words.

Now I have a list of events for you today.

1. You know that couple I mentioned a while back? The ones that play the "V" instrument. (I still don't know what it is.) Well, their names are Ricky and Helena Wood, and they tried to teach me how to read music last evening. All the boarders and Mrs. West sat in the parlor and watched as if I'm some sort of spectacle. Helena even let me try playing her "V" instrument. Oh, the screeching was *horrific.* It sounded like I was murdering a mouse. Will was chuckling the entire time. Karl was groaning. His mother was trying to smile and encourage me, but she looked in pain. Mrs. West left to "fetch tea," but I think she went up to bed and stuffed cotton balls in her ears. I shall never be a musician, I'm afraid. That dream has hit the road ... so I say, *auf wiedersehen, au revoir,* and good riddance.

2. I'm no longer a seamstress. That darling shop went out of business last week. Before you get worried, thinking I don't have a job, read on.

3. You'll be happy about this one ... I think. I got a job at Carnegie Hall. Yes, you read that right, but it's not what you think. I'm not *on* Carnegie Hall, though I desperately wish I was. I'm ... I'm cleaning it. Sweeping floors, dusting, washing windows. Bess! Can you believe it? I came to New York City and got

a job cleaning! I could do that anywhere! But don't fret. This is only temporary until I get a *real* job.

4. I can't escape Willoughby Reeves, and I can't say I mind it, though I am still embarrassed over numerous events. He got wind that I was working at Carnegie Hall (Mrs. West talks a lot) and came to see me! I was a mess after a full day of scrubbing dirt. My hair was a wreck—adorned with dust bunnies—and my dress was wrinkled. And I'm sure my mascara must have been smudged for I rubbed my eyes. I ran into him, quite literally, as I was leaving. He took off his hat while I gaped.

"Willoughby!" I squeaked.

"Georgiana," he said calmly.

"What are you doing here?" I asked loudly.

"Came to fetch you," he answered soothingly.

Our tones of voice are nothing alike. Ever.

"Fetch me? How odd. Why?" I scratched my head and felt a lump. Oh joy. Dust bunnies.

He stuffed his hands in his pocket and stared at me. "Want to go ice skating?"

Ice skating? Bess, I'd never gone ice skating before! It sounded … terrifying.

I hesitated while he kept staring at me. "I'd have to go get cleaned up … and I don't own skates … and

I'm quite scared to attempt it at all."

He waved away all my petty cares with a shake of his hand. "You look swell, we'll rent skates, and don't be sissy."

How's one to respond to *that?*

I felt like I was dripping in germs from cleaning the bathrooms. (*Yes. Bathrooms. Oh, Bess!*) I didn't say anything in reply for a long time. A gust of cold wind made me shiver and Will to hunch over, pulling his trenchcoat closer around himself. He waited patiently for me to speak. I was tired and wanted coffee (don't I always?), and so, I shook my head. "No, I don't think so."

I swear he read my thoughts, for the next thing he said was, "Hey, I'll buy you coffee."

Well, that's a different story.

"Really? Can you afford that? I don't drink one cup, you know."

"Yeah, I know." He grinned.

"All right then," I shrugged.

We walked toward the skating rink, the snow crunching under our feet. The city looked like it had been trapped in a snow globe. Big, fluffy flakes landed on my eyelashes, and I felt compelled to tilt my head up and catch them on my tongue. So I did.

Will stopped walking when he realized I wasn't next to him any longer. I was completely in my own little world, watching the flakes dance through the slate gray sky and feeling the iciness touch my skin. When I came back down to earth again, my stomach did a flip. Will had been staring at me the entire time with a little grin on his face. I'm sure my face looked like I had painted it with red acrylic.

"Onward?" I said, swiftly looking at my feet and hurrying down the road. He had to take long steps to catch up with me. The ice skating rink glistened in the sunlight, and it looked so smooth and … cold. I was able to rent a pair of skates, but they were a pain to put on. They squeezed my toes horribly. I'm rather scared to look at them now.

Now, normally I wouldn't hold hands with a young man unless we were … a couple. But I would have fallen flat on my face and cried like a baby if I didn't have Will to steady me. My ankles felt as if they'd snap under me. I was so afraid of falling that I gripped my fingers around his hands with all my strength. I'm sure I left marks.

"You're doing great," he said. "Just move your feet slowly."

I tried, Bess. I did. But have you ever felt complete slipperiness (I just made that word up because it suits) under your feet? It's not pleasant! I lost my footing, and my skate slid behind me, dragging me down to the cold ice with a *plop!*

Will grabbed my wrists and pulled me to my feet in one quick motion. "Are you all right?" he asked.

"Never better," I said, smiling at him.

He laughed, and so did I. When I looked at him, my heart flip-flopped … like a fish on land. That's not a very romantic simile, is it? I don't have a way with words … I apologize.

Well, after about an hour of skating, I subtly reminded him of his promise to buy me coffee. Did I subtly? Do I ever do things subtly? No. I recall telling him, "Coffee time."

He's a good sport. He nodded and said, "Yeah, I think you're right."

I think I'm starting to like this Willoughby fellow, even if his name is a little odd. But no teasing.

There are so many homeless on the streets, Bess. It makes me sad to look at them. I'm thankful that I have a roof over my head and a job, even if I have to clean bathrooms.

Your sister,

Gi

March 20th, 1936

Oh, Gi!

You must tone down on all this coffee intake! If you don't stop soon, you'll do something rash. What am I saying? You're always doing something rash.

Forgive me, but I believe you have just relayed to me the events of a date? A romantic date? May I be the first to tell Mama? I like this Willoughby fellow. I think he and I would get along very well. I wish you would come back home and bring him with you.

No. No, no, no! This is not how it's supposed to go, Gi. Tom and I are good friends. Nothing more, nothing less. We're like … we're like Jo and Laurie. Except I'm not much like Jo at all. I'm more of a Beth. Or … I blush as I say it, but almost like an Amy. Let's just drop this topic.

I'm curious, Gi. How did you get the job at Carnegie Hall? From the way you're talking, there are so many homeless in New York City that even jobs such as cleaning the bathrooms would be snatched up before you had a chance to get there.

Speaking of the homeless, I've seen three old trucks drive through here today. Trucks strapped with rickety old furniture and bundles of children. And downtrodden mothers and fathers, it appears. Gi, I'm frightened. What if that happens to us? We are already behind on payments at Mr. Yale's store. You knew that. What if we owe the bank money, and I don't know it? What if they take our house and our farm, and we have to leave? What if I never see Tom again?

Oh, Tom. I meant to tell you in the last letter, but I forgot. His grandfather doesn't like me. Every time I run across the road to their house, he vanishes from sight. For example, just this afternoon I skipped across to bring Tom back a book I borrowed from him. Old Mr. Thomas was sitting on the front porch and saw me coming. Do you know what he did? He got right up and walked into the house. And shut the door! I was so crushed I almost turned back around and hid in my bedroom. But Tom saw me from the upstairs window and opened it and waved. And climbed out the window onto the roof. And climbed off the roof into the tree. And swung down from the tree and landed a few feet in front of me. He's so cocky.

Isn't it perfectly awful? Not the cockiness— although he could stand to tone it down a bit—but the fact that old Mr. Thomas doesn't like me one bit. It's dreadful. I don't know what I am to do. What would you do?

I'm writing this letter from the front porch. It's pretty wretched out-of-doors right now, but it's more wretched indoors with nothing but candlelight and firelight. It's cold indoors, and it's cold out-of-doors, so at the moment, I'm taking the out-of-doors. I'm lying on my stomach on the front porch, and the wind keeps blowing the blanket off my shoulders. And it keeps blowing the paper from my hands, which is why it's stained with dust smudges. My apologies.

As you can see, nothing exciting has happened 'round here. Nothing ever does, really, although occasionally … just occasionally … I wish it would. What is the matter with me, Gi? Are you rubbing off on me? Or is it Tom? Sometimes I want to fly out the window, and I don't know why.

Your very confused sister who has stiff fingers from the cold,

Bess

March 26th, 1936

Dear Bess,

It was *not* a romantic date. He just wanted to laugh at my attempt to ice skate. Does that sounds romantic? But I do think you and Will would get along splendidly. I even think Papa might like Will more than he likes me!

You said it yourself, Bess. You are Amy, and Tom is Laurie. Have you read all of *Little Women* yet? Oh, what a surprise you're in for!

To answer your question about Carnegie Hall, Helena Woods got me the job. She and her husband know some of the big shots of the music world ... and believe it or not, there are still people who can afford going to concerts. I'm not getting full pay for cleaning ... that's why I can't send very much home ... and why I've cut back on my coffee. Helena told the managers that I'd take half of what they're paying one of their cleaners right now. You're right, of course. I shouldn't be complaining. I'm just a dreamer, Bess. Bathrooms are so unromantic.

The Depression is hitting NYC very hard, but I've been fortunate enough to avoid *most* of its unpleasantness. Today I saw a middle aged man with a hole in his hat. On his back was a sign that said:

I know three trades.

I speak three languages.

I fought for three years

Have three children

And no work for 3 months.

But I only want one job.

It makes me feel guilty for complaining about my job. There are a plethora of homeless shelters and soup kitchens. Will and I volunteered at a soup kitchen the other day. It made my heart sink to see little children so thin and homely.

But I'm still a dreamer, Bess. For some odd reason, I fancied myself a poet the other day. I had a cup of tea, a pile of paper, and my trusty ol' typewriter sprawled on my desk. I don't know what I was thinking ... I guess since I'm living in NYC and there are all these huge publishing houses, I thought I'd have a chance. *Ha!*

My poem:

Spring in the air,
My skin is very fair.
The grass is turning green.
I wish I was a queen.
The flowers are blooming,
And my land lady's voice is booming,
"Toast and jam!"
Into the food I slam.
It tastes very good.
I should stop writing poems, I should.
So I will.
And I like a lad named Willoughby.
There is nothing that rhymes with Willoughby.
The End.

Ha ... ha ... ha. I would have been mortified to show this to anyone but you ... but I did show it to Will. Here's how our conversation went:

Me: "I don't suppose you'd like to read the dumbest poem in the world?"

Will: "Sometimes I enjoy reading dumb poems."

Me: "Great. Read mine."

Will, after looking it over and trying not to laugh: "Oh, wow. Nice ... Gi ... nice."

That's when I remembered the stupid line at the bottom. *I like a lad named Willoughby.* And he was reading it. Willoughby was reading it! What was I thinking?!

Will: "I really like the last two lines."

I think I let out a screech right about then and tore it from his hands.

Me: "I ... that's not ... um ... you see ... *agh!*"

Will: "I said I *like* it. Why are you sputtering like a teapot?"

I tried smiling, but it was more like a grimace.

Me: "It's just a poem, you know. It doesn't mean anything."

Will, looking a little down in the dumps: "Oh."

I ripped the poem into shreds and tossed it in the fire. There. No proof that I had said anything about liking a lad named Willoughby. *Phew!*

The next evening after supper, all of the boarders retired to the parlor. Karl was talking and talking and talking … I glazed over, then saw a hand move back and forth in front of my face. It was Will's hand.

"Want to go dancing?" he said.

That snapped me back to reality. "Dancing? I can't!" You know how I wave my hands while I'm talking? Well, I ended up slapping poor Will in the face while trying to explain to him that I can't dance.

He rubbed his jaw where I had struck him and said, "Why not? Anyone can dance. Even me."

"I'm the exception."

"I don't believe you."

"*Believe me.* You'll be sorry. Your toes will be pancakes."

He made a face at that. "What a strange thing to say."

"I say a lot of strange things."

"Yeah, you do." He grinned. "So … are we dancing? I'll risk toe-like-pancakes, no matter how disgusting that sounds."

I busted a gut laughing at that. "Oh … I *guess* I could try. It might be fun … but we can't go looking like this."

I was still wearing my dull, faded pink work dress, and my hair was knotted over my shoulders. He was wearing suspenders and a white button-up shirt with the sleeves rolled up over his elbows. "Why not?"

"I look like a crazy woman!"

"And I look like a crazy man. Perfect!" He pulled me to my feet.

"You won't be embarrassed by me?" I asked skeptically.

"Never. You look swell."

That's when I realized we were still holding hands. I let go, and he cleared his throat. Someone had to say something, or we'd be stuck in this awkward trance forever!

"Well, shall we go?" I said.

"Yes." He nodded and fetched my jacket.

Now, Will is a journalist and makes a fair share of money, but nothing to brag about. That's why I couldn't believe it when we arrived at a classy, expensive-looking dancing hall.

"I can't afford this!" I told him. "I hardly have enough money to live on!"

"It's a birthday gift," he said.

Bess, I had completely forgotten that it was my twenty-first birthday ... or that I had mentioned my birthday to him at all!

It was toe-tapping music when we walked in! And what fun! The spinning made me a little sick, but I didn't mind much. You know how the music always changes to a waltz in those Hollywood films shortly after a couple has arrived to the dance? That happened on cue. When I watched those films, I thought it was dopey the way the couple talked sentimentally to one another.

Thankfully, it wasn't like that with Will and me. I don't know *how* to talk sentimentally. I think he'd be thankful that I spared him. Instead, I told him about our farm, and about you and Tom, Donny, and Mama and Papa. He wants to meet you all. He told me about his brother who lives in *Germany*. As in Europe. *Across the ocean.* He's an uncle to three—two nephews and one niece. He also has a younger brother and younger sister who live in Maine with his parents.

I learned quite a lot about him tonight. He has a better memory than I do.

– Gi

P.S. Don't worry over Mr. Thomas. I don't understand how anyone couldn't like a sweet thing like you! Perhaps he's suffering from a toothache.

April 3rd, 1936

Dear Gi,

I'm so selfish. I can't even begin to describe how selfish I am. It's awful, Gi. Because I'm trying to be unselfish, I'm going to reply very conscientiously to all of your news in your last letter.

That was very kind of you and Will to help out at the soup kitchen. Was it your idea or Will's?

That was very kind of Mrs. Woods to give you that job. I understand now how grateful you are to clean the bathrooms. Is Carnegie Hall pretty? I think I saw a picture of it once, but I don't remember what it looks like. I bet Tom ten cents the other day that your work place was more magnificent than his school was. The bet didn't really turn out to be a bet, though, because he agreed with me.

Mark my words, Georgiana Rowland. Willoughby Reeves is very fond of you. He took you dancing for your birthday, spending who knows how much money in order to do so. Perhaps he's skipping breakfasts now. Perhaps you matter more than food to him. That's a very important thing to a man. Food. You should see Tom wolf down meals. The fact that Will might be skipping meals now because he took you dancing is a very touching thing. And the fact that he looked crestfallen when you said you didn't mean you liked him is just another certain indication that he is very fond of you. He wants you to be fond of him, too.

Now you are probably wondering why I mentioned being unselfish. It's because of Tom. Well, not exactly because of Tom, but because of the hobos. Let me explain.

I was helping Mama by baking a loaf of bread in the kitchen the other day. It was a peaceful day. Strong breezes blew through the open window over the sink; it's finally becoming a little warmer out.

Anyway, I was absentmindedly mixing dough when Tom came storming into the kitchen, dragging Donny by the arm. "Did you tell him?" Tom demanded fiercely.

I was so surprised by his tone of voice that I dropped my spoon on the floor and stared at him.

Tom rolled his eyes in exasperation, rubbing his hands through his tousled red hair. "Did you tell him that hobos are wild, dangerous people?"

I backed up, bumping into the counter, as Tom strode toward me. I had never seen his eyes so on fire before, Gi. It was frightening. What was especially frightening was that he was angry at *me*. Tom's the last person on earth whom I'd think would get angry at me. My eyes welled up with tears then, Gi. Call me a baby, but I couldn't help it.

Next thing I knew, Tom was stroking my shoulder saying, "C'mon, Bess, don't cry. It's not ... well, what I mean is ... did you tell Donny that hobos are dangerous? 'Cause it's not true. Not all hobos are dangerous. That's why I got so upset. Aw, Bess, please don't cry." He used his wheedling voice then, and it worked. I stopped crying.

I got the hiccups then. Tom called me "Hiccup" for the rest of the day.

After I stopped crying, Tom brushed the tears off my cheeks, and the three of us—Tom, Donny, and me —all sat down at the table, and Tom rested his chin in his fists. That's one example of what I mean by boyish, Gi. When he sits like that, he has the freckled face of a seven-year-old rather than a seventeen-year-old.

"I know some hobos," Tom said slowly. "I knew some, anyway. I still do. But I knew some very well. And before we get any further, can we stop calling them hobos? They're people, too. They're just homeless. You got that?"

Donny and I nodded.

"Gi told me to watch out for hobos—homeless people—because they were on the loose," I told him. "That's why I told Donny they're dangerous. I thought she meant they were."

"Gi's ignorant on that topic," he said ruthlessly. I was rather hurt by that comment. But I kept my mouth shut.

"Have you been down to the railroad tracks?" Tom asked me.

"No," I said in confusion. "You mean the ones a few miles out of town?"

He did. He said there were close to ten little tents and shacks set up down there. I didn't believe him at first. But then he took Donny and me down to see it. If you could have seen all those people, Gi! There were little children! Mothers with babies. There were structures set up made of nothing but ragged strips of cloth or cardboard. It was awful. These people lived there. It may be starting to become April, but it's still cold. And many of them were sick.

"What is this place?" I whispered to Tom, holding tightly to Donny's hand.

"It's a Hooverville," Tom explained, striding forward ahead of Donny and me.

A Hooverville, he explained later, was a shanty town set up by the homeless. There are ones much, much bigger in New York, he told me. I could have cried. Have you seen a Hooverville, Gi?

Donny and I stood uncomfortably watching the activity of the homeless people. Tom was now standing outside a canvas tent, his foot resting on a wooden crate, as he talked gravely with a poor woman who held a silent babe in her arms. I glanced down at Donny and then grabbed his hand and tugged him toward Tom. But Tom had turned and was walking toward us.

"C'mon, Hiccup," he said, looking me in the eye. "This little guy needs some milk desperately. He's weak. And sick, pretty bad. Can you take him while I escort Mrs. Harvey to Grampa's? I told her that Grampa might have something she can do in order to get some."

"Why doesn't your grampa just give it to her?" I whispered to him, glancing at the tired-looking lady.

"Because, Bess," Tom said patiently, shoving his hands in his pockets as he gazed at Mrs. Harvey with sadness in his pale blue eyes. "Most people can't bear charity."

"How come?"

"Dignity. Pride. Even if you've lost it all, that's somethin' you can hold onto."

"That and Jesus," I said and then realized I sounded like a prissy Sunday school girl. But Tom just smiled and nodded, repeating, "That and Jesus."

So Tom beckoned to Mrs. Harvey, who joined us and handed me her baby. Nathaniel, his name is. He's a precious little fellow, but his cheeks were burning with fever. And his breathing was so wheezy, Gi. I feared he'd choke on his own breath.

Donny wanted to hold him, too, so I let him. But when Nathaniel started coughing violently, I tore him right out of Donny's arms. It was a scary moment.

After about an hour—a very long hour—Mrs. Harvey returned with a little pail of milk. Mr. Thomas had instructed her to wash their front porch, she said. There was happiness in her voice. I wondered how someone like her could feel something like happiness when her babe was sick, and she didn't know where her next meal was coming from. Tom said she doesn't know where her husband is either. Oh, Gi, isn't it perfectly awful? I feel so much pain for that woman.

Anyhow, I'm sorry for conveying such distressing news to you. But it's sticking to my heart like glue, and sometimes it hurts too badly to run through my own head. I have to write it on paper and know that you'll read it and listen.

Give Will my love. I really mean that. I want to see what he says in response.

Your somber sister,

Bess

P.S. I have not finished *Little Women* yet. I finished the first half while I was laid up with a swollen ankle, but the second part has yet to be read. What do you mean by saying I am up for a surprise? I'm a little wary now.

April 10th, 1936

Bess,

I'm the selfish one. Not you. You've never been selfish ... you're always so patient and kind with Donny ... always thinking of him first. Of course it wasn't my idea to help at the soup kitchen. I wouldn't have thought of something so unselfish and *good*. I'm very glad that Will has such a tender heart. I forget to help others most times. But I'm going to change that, Bess. I want to be unselfish and humble. I really do!

But allow me one last moment to wallow in self-pity.

I must quote Anne Shirley because she says it so well: I am in the depths of despair! I cried all night. My face is red, and my eyes are puffy this morning. It doesn't matter. I don't have anywhere to go anyway.

I lost my job. Someone else came along who'd accept less pay. Of course, it makes financial sense for the managers to snatch up someone whom they could pay less to do the same work. I looked all over NYC to find another job ... but there aren't any. And to make matters worse, Will is leaving. He's going to cover stories of "the dust bowl aftermath in the midwest" for the newspaper. How could life go from simply smashing to so gloomy in a matter of days?

I thought NYC was grand a few days ago. Now it feels rather hellish. Mama would be horrified that I wrote hellish. But that's how it feels. I've been very good about saving my money and not wasting it on petty things (like coffee), so I'm all set for now.

Will's leaving one week from today. *Sob!* He did something very sweet for me yesterday. He was going to take me to a Broadway show.

"You can't afford that!" I told him.

"I've been saving my money just for this occasion." He smiled. "Ever since I bumped into you at the last Broadway show. I was there on business doing a review and you—as you recall—were sneaking in."

"Yes, I remember that very vividly. But Will, that's *so* much money!" I thought of what a help that money would be to you at home. "I can't," I said.

"Why not?"

"I can't when my family is struggling. It doesn't seem right."

He was quiet for a long moment and then smiled. "You're right. I have another idea." He reached into his pocket and handed me a wad of cash—the cash for the tickets. I believe you're right when you mentioned he must be skipping meals. "Send this to your family … and how about we go for a walk instead? I just wanted to spend time with you before I leave."

I refused. I held both hands behind my back and shook my head defiantly. "That's very charitable of you, but—"

"It's not charity."

I laughed at that. "Then what is it?"

"It's … "

"See! You think I need charity. Well, I don't."

"Gi, just take it for heavens sake. We don't have all day to fight about money."

I shook my head. "I won't take it."

A mixture of anger and annoyance blazed in his eyes. He grabbed my hand and pried my fist open, attempting to place the cash into my palm. "Gi, don't be stubborn."

I pulled my hand back.

"This is ridiculous." He stared me down, and I was starting to feel sheepish. If only he didn't look so stern!

"Yes, it is ridiculous. Put the cash back in your pocket like a good fellow and let's take a stroll." I took a step forward, my chin held high.

"What about your family? Don't you think they need the money? Are you going to let your pride deprive them of food?"

I glanced over my shoulder at him. "My pride?" I was ready to fight this out.

He must have sensed that I was getting riled up for his voice grew calmer. "All right, Gi. If you won't send this to them, I'll ransack your letters and find their address myself."

He would do it. I knew he would. I swallowed my pride and slowly held out my hand. "Oh … very well." He placed the money in my palm and closed my fingers around it with a smile. "Thank you," I said. "I will pay you back."

He didn't say anything in response. He probably didn't want to get into another argument.

And that's why you now hold a good sum of money in your hands. I don't know how I'll ever repay him.

We went walking, avoiding Central Park, even though it looks lovely this time of year. It seems to be a place for "dangerous" people to gather. Or at least, that's what I've heard.

"Central Park is so beautiful! Look at all the flowers and the trees in full bloom!" I said as we passed it.

Will stopped walking and placed both hands on my shoulders, looking into my eyes. "Gi, promise me you'll never go in there by yourself."

I laughed at him. "You worry too much!"

His gaze grew even more intense. "Gi."

"All right. I promise," I said. I don't know if it's *truly* dangerous, but I made a promise to Will that I won't break. He seemed content with my answer, and so, we continued walking. "You'll be so far away," I said after a moment.

"I know." He glanced at me. "Do you ever think of moving back to Kansas?"

"No," I scoffed, stepping over a puddle.

"Why not?"

"Because I couldn't stand it. My father didn't want me to move to New York. If I come back now without any money or prospects, he'll say, 'I told you so.' I'll never live it down."

"You and your father don't get along, I'm guessing?"

"Not at all."

"Same thing happened to me. My old man thought I was insane to go into journalism. He thought I should follow the family trade of being a fisherman, like him. We had a huge fight, and that's when I moved to New York." He stopped talking for a moment as we squeezed through a crowd. Will grabbed my hand and pulled me close as we struggled through. When we had reached a clear patch of sidewalk, we should have let go of one other's hands. But we forgot.

"My old man had a heart attack a year later. Almost killed him," Will went on. "I took the first train back to Maine and prayed so hard that I'd make it in time. God answered my prayers, and I made it. He was bedridden, so I sat next to his bed all that day and talked to him. We made our peace with each other, and he ended up recovering. But I wouldn't have been able to forgive myself if he died and the last thing I called him was—well, never mind."

"So you're saying I should make peace with my father? But Will, he just *doesn't* understand me!"

"All the more reason to talk with him, Gi."

Well, that was something to chew on. I'm still chewing. It doesn't taste good.

Next thing he said was, "Remember when I offered a job to you, back when you drank ten cups of coffee?"

He has a habit of bringing up my embarrassing moments. "Yes."

"Would you like to hear it now?"

"I suppose."

"I need a photographer," Will said. "I have one now, but he's no good. I'm ready to replace him … with you." He looked at me and grinned.

"Me? A photographer?"

"Yeah, why not?"

"Because I've never held a camera in my life!"

"That doesn't matter. It's how you see the world, Gi. You see it with bright, dream-filled eyes. That's what I need. That's what the world needs right now in the midst of this depression. But you'll have to move away from New York."

Here I was faced with two major life decisions, Bess. Take his offer of being a photographer with him out west, or stay in NYC and prove to the world that I could take care of myself. I know which one I should have chosen now. I should have taken his offer. But I didn't.

I thought of what your Tom said about the hobos. He's right you know. They're people, too. I didn't mean that they were all bad, Bess. I just didn't think it was wise for you to be outside all alone at night. I'm rather protective of my younger siblings, you know.

Your description of Hooverville made my heart sting, Bess. I have seen one in NYC. I cried the entire way home. This city is so strange. There's wealth and pleasure, but also poverty and despair right next to it. I once wrote that I was having a "great time during this Great Depression." It's no longer true.

I told Will that you send your love. Here's what he said:

"You've been writing to her about me?"

"Just a little."

He nodded his head. "That's nice. Tell her I send my love, too. And I send my love to Donny and your parents. Tell her that I hope I can meet her someday … and pick on her."

He's very good at picking on people. So watch out.

What do you suppose Tom would say if I sent my love to him?

– Gi

April 15th, 1936

Oh, Gi.

I'm so sorry. I'm so sorry about Will leaving. I'm so sorry about your losing your job. But I think you'll understand completely when I tell you that you are absolutely stupid, Georgiana Rowland. Why did you not take Will's job? You would be with Will. You would have a job. You would be coming back home to the dear, wild West! I don't understand you at all. You're so stubborn sometimes.

But the money you sent us. Oh, Gi! I swear I saw Papa's eyes mist up when I brought it to him. Don't you see? Papa's proud of you. I think you could get along well if only you'd both get over your differences.

I told Tom you sent your love. I wasn't going to at first. But we were sitting in their upper sitting room. They've turned it into a library, Gi. It's the most beautiful, cozy, homey room. The walls are covered with books. Novels, historicals, biographies, atlases. It's a heaven on earth, in my opinion. Anyhow, I was curled up in a big stuffed chair reading *Little Women*, and he was sprawled on the floor studying an atlas. It was so homey and comfortable. I remembered your letter and looked down at him. I studied him a moment. Then I said, "Gi sends her love." Tom looked up at me in surprise. "Really?" he asked, searching my eyes. "Have you told her about me?"

"Of course!" I laughed a little and went back to my book. My cheeks felt so hot I was sure they were bright red. I didn't dare look back at him the rest of the afternoon.

He walked me across the street come dinnertime. It was dark then. I would have walked myself just fine. I'd done it many times before. But he insisted on escorting me. We strolled across slowly and walked up the steps to the porch. Just before I went inside, Tom caught my arm. "Tell Gi I send my love, too," he said, smiling.

I smiled back at him. I couldn't help it. "Well," he said, "goodbye." And he walked back across the road, his hands shoved in his pockets. I watched him for a second. Then I went back inside and flew up to my room, crashing on my bed.

His hand was shaking, Gi. When he caught my arm.

That's the most news I have from here. Not much has happened lately. Oh, Donny's sick. Poor little fellow's got a fever. I think it might be from holding little Nathaniel several days ago. He's sleeping in Mama's bed right now. I hope he feels better soon. I want to take him out to the swimming hole—I mean, mudhole. There are some pretty little white flowers growing in around it. I haven't seen flowers like that in a long, long time.

I'm sending prayers your way, o stubborn sister of mine.

Love,

    Bess

April 19th, 1936

Dear Bess,

Thank you for your sympathy, even if you did call me stupid. *I* can call myself stupid, but knowing you think I'm stupid isn't a pleasant thought to dwell on. I know I'm stubborn. I can't help it, Bess! It's a horrible flaw I must endure ... or overcome ... whichever comes first.

I wish I could believe that Papa was proud of me. But what's there to be proud of? It was Will who made that money, not me. Does Papa talk about me at all? Is he in good health?

I'm awfully glad that Tom sends his love, the dear boy. I'd like to meet him, Bess. But that would mean coming home, wouldn't it? I wish you, Tom, and Donny could visit me ... but that would be a dull time since I have no extra money. Speaking of Donny, send him my love and tell him he *must* get better ... Gi's orders.

Well, Bess, I said goodbye to Will at the train station today. It was horrible. No, not just the fact that he was leaving me. There were a few other things.

We walked together to the station, and I was wearing those old hand-me-down heels. They've been hand-me-downed too many times. The heel snapped on the left shoe and sent me sprawling to the ground. I'm the most ungraceful woman on this planet, Bess! Will was exclaiming (through his laughter ... I must have looked funny), "Gi, are you okay?"

I held up my shoe with the heel dangling by a thread. "My best pair of shoes," I said mournfully.

He helped me up (this is getting to be a habit: Will helping me up) and looked at the shoe. "I might have a stick of chewing gum in my suitcase ... I could chew it and stick the heel back on with it. Should I check?" His eyes were dancing with mischief.

"No!" I yanked off my other shoe. "I'll walk barefoot. Save your gum for another emergency."

Well, I *thought* I'd walk barefoot. The sidewalk was peppered with little stones, dirt, and a variety of unrecognizable particles that stabbed into my poor feet. I haven't walked barefoot since last autumn. My feet are beginning to be sissies. "Ouch. *Ouchouchouch!*" was what I said the entire time.

Will turned and looked at me. "Gi, you look as if you're walking over burning coals."

I was about to throw my heel at him, but he had already whisked me off my feet. Before I knew what was happening, I was being carried by Willoughby Reeves through the streets of New York. I had to wrap my arms tightly around his neck and hang on for dear life, for he was also carrying his suitcase. What a spectacle we must have been!

That was the first thing that went wrong.

When we arrived at the station, we stood around for a spell and waited for his train to arrive. We were outside, welcoming the warm breezes on our faces. I could hear birds singing to us from above. (They were really plotting against me.) I was wearing my best coral dress when a bird left a dropping on my shoulder. It seeped through my sleeve, and I could feel the warmth on my skin. I let out a screech which caused Will to turn quickly and hit his head on the ticket sign.

"Are you okay?" we both exclaimed at the same time.

"*A bird pooped on me!*" I cried.

"I hit my head on this stupid sign," he groaned. "Did it leave a mark?"

While I was inspecting his head to see if there was a dent, he was fishing in his pocket for a handkerchief to give me.

That was the second thing that went wrong.

After I assured him that there wasn't a dent on his head, and when my shoulder was free of bird droppings, the train pulled in. We stared at each other as the train puffed circles of smoke behind us. The ticket master was calling for everyone to board.

"Will we ever see each other again?" I asked.

"What a thing to ask!" he laughed. "Of course we will."

"But ... *when?*"

"Soon. Maybe I'll be reassigned to New York. Or maybe you'll decide to move out west." He grinned.

The train whistle blew and rattled my brain. It's so annoyingly loud. Will set down his suitcase and wrapped his arms around me. We hugged for a long moment, then he pulled away slowly. Only, my head was attached ... to his. My hair clip had snagged on his hair, and there we stood, stuck together.

"All aboard!" the ticket master yelled.

"Uh ... coming!" Will shouted, trying to free himself from my head. "Gi, do you have gum in your hair or something?"

"No! It's a clip."

My hair is so knotted that it snags on things extremely easily ... but you know that already, Bess. Remember when you tried brushing it that one time and the brush got anchored to my head? It was like that. We weren't getting anywhere. Either I'd have to get on the train with him, or he'd have to miss it.

"Okay, on the count of three, we'll pull," Will said. "One, two, *three.*"

We pulled away from each other, but that only caused us to wince in pain. We were still stuck.

That's when we had to call on a stranger to help us. It was a young lady who heard our cry for help. She hurried over and tried freeing us.

"I've got a pair of scissors in my purse," she said. Then she snipped us free, leaving me robbed of a few inches of hair on the right side.

We thanked her for her service, then she disappeared.

"Well, that was interesting," Will said, rubbing his head. "I suppose I shouldn't hug you again." So instead he grabbed my hand. "Take care of yourself, Gi."

"You too." And then—you'll be shocked at me, Bess —I kissed him. *I kissed Willoughby Reeves in public!* What would Papa say? He'd have a heart attack, I'm certain. Don't you dare tell him, Bess. It wouldn't be good for his health.

Will was quite stunned. "Georgiana Rowland, I'm floored."

"So am I," I said, nervously pushing a curl behind my ear. "You ... you better catch your train."

He smiled, slightly dazed as he backed away from me. I know he was dazed, for he bumped right into someone. Will never bumps into people. He's always aware of his surroundings.

"Sir! Are you boarding this train, or aren't ya?" the ticket master barked.

"Yes ... I am ... so sorry," Will stammered. I watched as he turned and hurriedly boarded the train. It inched out of the station, taking my Will with it.

I finally turned to leave, and that's when I noticed that my purse was gone. I panicked and searched around frantically. Had I dropped it on the way? My mind was whirling. I had money in there that I couldn't afford to have wander away. Could someone have stolen it? That's when an image popped into my head of a lady with scissors. How could someone have stolen it without me noticing unless they had snipped the strap?

There I stood, jobless, purseless, shoeless, Willoughbyless, and with a bird dropping stain on my shoulder.

Another night of crying for me.

– Gi

April 29th, 1936

Dearest Georgiana,

I'm so worried. I'm sorry I haven't written. I've been so full of emotion. I have so much to tell you. I must start from the beginning. Do you remember how I said Donny had a fever?

A couple of days after I sent your last letter, I was washing dishes before the open window in the kitchen. Priss sat on the counter watching me, mewing remorsefully whenever a splatter of water hit her nose. It was a lovely day.

Mama came running downstairs a moment later. "Donny's crying," she said. "He can't speak because of his throat, and he's got a violent red rash on his face."

Papa stood up slowly, his eyes widening. "Are you sure, Liz?" he asked her.

"Of course, I'm sure," Mama snapped. Mama never snaps, Gi. You know that.

Papa followed her upstairs. I stood rather frozen before the sink a moment. Then I dropped the pot I was washing with a clatter and ran upstairs. Priss followed me.

Papa was bending over the bed, his large palm covering Donny's forehead. "How do you feel?" he asked.

Donny shook his head, tears rolling down his flushed cheeks. He looked at me then. Oh, Gi! I cry as I recall it. He was begging me to help. To relieve his pain.

"Call the doctor, Papa," I said, grabbing Donny's chubby fists. Priss sprang softly on the bed, curling up next to Donny. His fingers reached for her as he buried his poor little face in her fur.

Papa stood up slowly. He nodded, and for the first time, I saw more than worry in his eyes. "It looks like scarlet fever," he said to us under his breath.

I lost my breath then. I almost smothered Donny, but Mama grabbed my arm. "Run for the doctor."

I did, Gi. I flew. I reached town and pounded on Doctor Murray's door. His wife answered. Said he was at the general store picking up a sack of flour for her. I high-tailed it down to the general store then.

There was so much hurt and fear raging in my chest, Gi. It was so sudden, and I had never felt anything like it before.

I pushed open the general store door and ran smack into a man. I sort of gasped and jumped back. I found myself staring up at a young stranger with very handsome dark eyes. He started to say he was sorry when I burst into tears and buried my face in his chest.

The man sort of stood stock still for a moment, and I sensed him turning his head around to look at Mr. Yale behind the counter. "I'm really sorry, kid," he said kindly, awkwardly stroking my hair.

"I'm Bess, Will," I said, stepping back and brushing my cheeks. I didn't realize he would be so tall. Or perhaps I'm shorter than I remembered.

Will sort of gaped at me for a moment and dropped his suitcase. He wrapped me in a hug then and said, "What's wrong, kiddo? Did I hurt you?"

"Donny's sick with scarlet fever." The words falling from my lips didn't feel like my own, and my eyes kept welling up with tears though I tried to stop them. Will's eyes grew wide, and he muttered, "Good God."

I ran toward Doctor Murray with Will on my heels and explained Donny's state to him. "Oh, dear God," he breathed, and I knew, Gi, that we needed prayers more than anything else right then.

The three of us hurried toward home after the doctor stopped at his house for his medical bag. We were pounding up the porch steps when Doctor Murray turned to look at us, barring the door with his arms. "If it really is scarlet fever," he said gravely, looking at Will in particular, "then this place must be quarantined. I shouldn't be allowing you to enter the house."

"To heck with quarantine," Will snapped and wrenched open the screen door. He tossed his suitcase on the sofa, and we both tore upstairs with Doctor Murray on our heels.

Mama and Papa looked up, startled, when we burst in. "What in the name—what's going on?" Papa growled at me.

"This is Willoughby Reeves, Papa," I said softly.

Papa looked taken aback and gazed at Will.

"How's the kid, sir?" There was so much concern in Will's voice, Gi! You would have fallen in love with him all over again. I know I did. I adopted him as my older brother right then and there.

Papa slowly held out his hand, and Will firmly shook it.

Doctor Murray cut in then and sent Will and me downstairs. I barely caught a glimpse of Donny as I went out the door, but he looked awful. It ignited the tears again, and I collapsed on the sofa downstairs, wrapping my arms around my knees and staring at the empty hearth. Will gazed at me a moment, I think, slowly rolling up his shirtsleeves. "Y'know," he said softly, "I felt the same when I was pitched the news that my old man'd had a heart attack."

"Yeah?" I whispered, looking at him. His brown eyes were so kind. I needed him just then.

"Do you feel like someone's slugged you in the stomach?" he asked, sitting down next to me on the sofa.

I inhaled, leaning my chin on my knees. "Yeah."

We were quiet for a moment.

"Y'know," Will said gently, gazing at me with sad eyes, "you and Gi look like sisters."

"Except the hair color," I sighed, touching the blond braids piled on my head. I missed you so much then, Gi. I needed you. I told Will that. Do you know what he said?

"Me too." He looked away, out the window. "Me too, Bessie."

There was a rap on the door just then, and I stumbled to open it. Tom stood there outside, a nervous smile on his face. "Hey," he said, clutching a piece of paper in his hands. "Want to go for a walk?"

I burst into tears again. I was such a mess, Gi. Sudden fear must do that to me.

Tom was alarmed. "What's going on, Bess?" he asked, grabbing my hands. The piece of paper fluttered away in the wind. "What's happened?"

"Donny's got scarlet fever," I wept. I didn't realize Will had followed me. Tom looked at him in confusion, and I didn't have the right frame of mind to introduce them. Somehow Will managed to explain who he was and what was going on. I sat down right in the front doorway and rocked back and forth. You can see now, I suppose, why I didn't write to you sooner. I've been a mess for days.

I caught the last of Will's words. "I guess you can't be here, considering it's supposed to be quarantined." They weren't rude words. They were apologetic. But Tom looked crushed all the same. He looked down at me. He looked down at his empty hands. Then he crouched down next to me, pressed my palm and said, "I'm so sorry, Bess. I'm so, so sorry." I think his eyes were filling with tears.

Then he leapt off the porch and ran back across the road. Will bent down next to me and kissed my hair, saying, "C'mon, Bessie. I'll stay awhile. Kinda have to, I guess. We're all quarantined in here and all."

Will's been our rock for many days. Donny's still not out of the thick of the fever, but I think—I hope—I *pray* it's waning. All that to say, I wish you'd taken Will's job and come home, Gi. I wish you had.

I miss you.

With love,

Bess

May 5th, 1936

Bess,

You sure know how to throw complete and utter surprise on a person! I cried and was an absolute baby as I read your letter. Donny! I can't stand this, Bess! I can't stand knowing he's so sick, and there's nothing I can do to help him! Oh, Bess! My tears are staining this letter. Please know how much my heart aches for you all.

And this business of running into Will! How did you know it was him? For a moment, I thought you must be seeing things. Of all the places for Will to end up, it couldn't be Kansas. But then I received a letter from him shortly after your's came. I can almost picture you two sitting at our kitchen table writing letters together. Perhaps you've even read his letter ... if not, here's what it says:

Dear Gi,

You won't believe it. I'm certain you won't. I can picture you now, eyes wide and mouth agape, when I tell you. Are you in suspense yet, or should I drag this on a bit longer?

(Then he goes on to talk about trivial things just to make me mad.)

I've just finished having supper with your family. Yes, you read that right. I ran into (quite literally) your sister at the general store. She was crying. I had no idea who this girl was, but after I had a good look at her, I knew. Good Lord, you two are the spitting image of one another. I told her so, too. Sweet girl, your sister is. And your brother … well, I'm sure Bessie told you already that he's sick. The kid will pull through, Gi. I know he will.

I think of you often … I wonder why you didn't take my job offer, Gi. I really wish you had. (So does your sister, by the way.) I think about running into you on Broadway and how embarrassed you looked. You don't know how nice you look when you're embarrassed. Then I think of the time you drank too much coffee. And when we went ice skating and dancing … I also think about the last time I saw you: barefooted, bird poop on your shoulder, and hair a mess from being stuck to my head. You looked beautiful, Gi. You stole my breath away. I mean it.

Have I made you blush yet? Good. But don't let it go to your head.

Yours affectionately,

Will

P.S. Bessie's boyfriend (she insists he's not, but I'm not so sure) is a nice kid. I've taken on the big brother role, and I'm making sure Tom deserves your sister. So far, I think he does. But maybe I'll have him run the gauntlet, just to be sure ... you know, make sure he's a man and all. I'll keep an eye on those two for you.

I'm so extremely grateful that Will is with you during this horrible time. I dearly wish I was there to comfort you, Bess. I would hop a train and come right away, only, I don't have enough money. Why didn't I go with Will? Why didn't I take the photography job? I could kick myself for being so stupid!

In other news, my rent was due last week, and I was afraid that I wouldn't have enough money. Thankfully I got another job. It's nothing glamorous. Actually, it's about as distant to glamorous as you can possibly get. It's washing dishes at a smelly seafood restaurant. The smell of seafood makes me sick to my stomach! I'm there all day, scrubbing crusty fish off crusty plates. I leave smelling like fish. It's the most disgusting thing I've ever endured! They have coffee that I'm allowed to drink. It tastes like fish.

We also have three new borders. I met them last night at supper. Bess, they give me the heebie-jeebies! There are two men and one woman. One man has a handle-bar mustache and dark eyes. The other is clean-shaven and bald. The woman is skinny and has frightfully long fingernails painted blood red. You know that I'm usually welcoming of anyone, but I think I'm seeing things in darker hues these past few weeks.

I desperately miss you, Donny, Mama, Will, and yes, maybe even Papa. Well, I better wrap this letter up. It's nearly eight, and I need to get to work. A pile of dishes awaits.

Please keep me updated on Donny's health. Write as soon as you can, for I long to hear from you.

– Gi

May 10th, 1936

Gi,

Donny's going to be well! Doctor Murray has told me he's certain of it, which generally means it's very certain. I jumped on Will's back when we found out, and I choked him, and he spun me onto the sofa.

As you see, we've become quite good friends. He's like a big brother I never had. I hope you keep him.

(Also, I'm really not sure how I knew it was Will. I just knew. Have you ever just *known* something you shouldn't be able to know?)

A few hours ago, when we first received your letters, I had just awoken and was still in my pajamas and robe; Will's hair was a mess, but at least he was freshened up for the day. Anyway, Tom had rapped on the kitchen window then, his face anxious.

"Mail for you," he shouted through the glass, saluting to us.

"Thank you, sire," I said, smiling, as I opened it a crack, and he slipped the letters in.

"Wait!" he said, just as I began to close it.

"What?"

"I miss you, Bess."

"Really?" I kind of froze up then. I don't know what got into me. He stared at me so sadly, his pale blue eyes very remorseful. I think it was the same way Will must have looked at you when—oh, never mind.

"What's 'run the gauntlet' mean?" I asked Will, as we sat across from one another at the kitchen table, drinking up your letters.

"The devil!" Will exclaimed, clapping his hand to his heart. "Did that woman go and copy my letter into yours?" He played up a dramatic scene that seemed quite Romeo and Juliet.

I teased him by saying, "No. Why?"

I must have done a good job because he looked really sheepish.

Then I said, "Yup," because I cannot lie. I'm pretty sure if I did, my nose would grow three feet and four inches, and I would no longer be able to get into the refrigerator. Which would be a pity, for milk is my favorite.

Will groaned and laid his palm on his letter. "Do you know what she sent me?"

"No, what?"

"Not telling." Will sent me a saucy smile and slipped out of his seat, sliding your letter into his breast pocket and pouring himself a glass of milk. Foul man. I like him. I think that ...

May 12, 1936

Tom has a habit of interrupting my letters. I write this with tears in my eyes. There, one just spotted the page. I'm sorry, Gi.

Will didn't have to make Tom run the gauntlet. He came out and told me so this morning. And I was there. I saw everything.

I cut off writing yesterday, as you noticed, I'm sure. I was peacefully writing your letter at my desk in front of the bedroom window, one eye on the page and one eye on Tom's house across the street, as I always do. I saw the front door burst open. Tom and a woman bolted out and tore down the street and out of sight. I had just enough time to catch the terror written on their faces.

And I recognized the woman. It was Mrs. Harvey, from the Hooverville by the railroad tracks. (By the way, I have a deep, deep fear of railroad tracks now.)

I froze one second, my pen up in the air. Then, with a sudden strike of the same thing in me that induces wanderlust, I slid open my window, climbed out on the porch, and slid down the tree. Then I tore down to the Hooverville.

Recalling now, I remember how absolutely lovely it was to be out in the open spring air. (Not that I was barred from it completely during this quarantine. A couple nights ago, Will woke me up and said we should rebel and go outside. So we did.)

I reached the Hooverville, my heart throbbing in my ears. But it was rather what I had expected. Tom stood by Mrs. Harvey's shack. His face was pinched with pain as he clutched little Nathaniel in his arms.

I ran over to him, hardly noticing Mrs. Harvey's weeping. "What's wrong?" I asked him, my eyes welling up with tears.

"Go get Doctor Murray," Tom said quietly. He didn't snap. He merely spoke calmly and quietly to me, and the dead serious tone of his voice spurred my feet to fly. I had never heard him so solemn before.

It was a very *déjà vu* moment, for I pounded on Doctor Murray's door and was informed that he was again at the general store. I slammed into the general store, ignoring the horrified stares of everyone. They knew I was quarantined, of course. Everyone knew.

"What is it, child?" the doctor asked me in alarm, when I found him jovially playing checkers with Mr. Yale at the front counter. "Don't tell me it's Donny?"

"No, sir," I gasped, hugging my chest. "It's a baby."

"A baby?" he inquired, his brow furrowing. "What do you mean?"

"A baby in the Hooverville."

Doctor Murray's brows raised sky-high, and he began to ask more questions, but I whimpered, "Oh, please come. Tom's got the baby now."

So he came.

And when we reached the Hooverville, Mrs. Harvey was nowhere to be seen. Tom still clutched the little child in his strong arms. Perspiration clung to his face when we reached him, and he muttered, "It's too late."

"W-what?" I said, freezing in my tracks.

"It was scarlet fever, doctor," Tom said, standing up. I noticed he was trembling. "I should have known. Oh, dear God, I should have known."

"What are you saying?" I whispered, as Doctor Murray slowly took the baby in his arms. I didn't glance at Nathaniel. I couldn't bring myself to do so. Instead, I stared at Tom's broken face as Nathaniel was taken away from us. From his mother. From this world.

I fell on my knees, and Tom slowly sat on the crate again as Doctor Murray went to find Mrs. Harvey. Tom's hands hung limply over his knees, and the very fact that he was staring numbly into space shook me all the more. I tugged on his arm, saying, "Tom, what do you mean you should have known?"

"More ways than one, Bess," Tom said, pulling away. He ran his hands through his hair, and I realized he was tearing at it in agony. He kept swallowing and swallowing, like he was trying to escape something inside of him, and it wasn't working at all. Finally he said, "I bet you wondered how I knew so much about Hoovervilles."

I said nothing. I just laid my head on his knees in exhaustion. He stroked my hair and said, "I was a hobo once, Bess."

"Really?" I said softly, gazing into the dirt.

"Yeah." Tom didn't say anything for a long moment. Finally he said, "Then my mother and father died."

"Oh."

"They died of scarlet fever. When I was twelve, they got very sick. I didn't know much about sickness, but I knew I needed a doctor to help them.

But I couldn't afford one. I didn't even know I had a grampa, actually, until after they'd ... they'd died." Tom stopped stroking my hair, and I looked up after a moment. Tears were streaming down his dirty, freckled cheeks. He rubbed them away impatiently, but they kept coming. He couldn't stop crying, Gi. That made me cry, and I knew he hated that, but I couldn't help it. Death makes me cry. I hate the end of things, especially the end of life on earth. I know that heaven is much, much better, but missing someone hurts too badly.

I hate it.

"You know," Tom said, swallowing and trying to wipe the tears off my cheeks. "I should have known."

"Should have known what?" I sniffed, looking up at him. My knees were beginning to hurt from kneeling in the dust.

"Should have known that Donny had caught whatever Nathaniel ... had." Tom started breathing heavily, looking up at the sky. "I should have known better than to bring you and Donny here. I should have *known* that Donny had what Nathaniel had. I should have known, then, at least, that Nathaniel had scarlet fever. And if I had known that—"

"Shut up!" I burst into tears all over again. "Don't blame yourself, Tom! God knew what He was doing!"

Tom looked at me and then wrapped his arms around my shoulders. I cried into his shoulder.

What happened next is all a blur to me, Gi, but I'll try to explain it as well as I can to you.

There was a train at the station at the time. It was a freight train. (Meaning it carried supplies, not people.) There was not much in the boxcars. Half of them were empty. Anyway, the train howled, announcing its departure. All the cars were further up toward the station at the time because the Hooverville is further out of town than the station. But we could see the engine of the train because it was facing our direction. It was facing west.

And Tom's clutch on my shoulders suddenly pinched because he saw Mrs. Harvey begin running toward it. Then he practically pushed me back and started running toward her.

And I started running after him, rather confused at what was happening.

The train began to move. It howled again, and then it creaked, and then the big, heavy cars started moving. And the engine started rolling toward us. Mrs. Harvey was running toward the moving train;

Tom was running toward Mrs. Harvey; and I was running toward Tom. I couldn't believe my eyes when I saw Mrs. Harvey grab hold of the ladder outside a boxcar and slip inside.

That's when I caught up to Tom. He had stopped abruptly. "What is she doing?" I cried.

"Catching a ride," he said, suddenly turning around and running along the railroad tracks. And I ran with him. Because the train had been moving slower than us at first, we were ahead of it.

But the train was starting to pick up speed.

"What are you doing?" I hollered.

"Following her!" Tom said, breathing heavily.

I ran right along with him. "I'm coming with you!" I cried.

"No, you don't know how to do it!" Tom said, grabbing my arm and pushing me away from the tracks.

I tumbled into the dirt. "Then how do you know?" I screamed, scrambling back up. The train's rumble was growing much louder, and I knew it was gaining on us.

"Because I've done it before!" Tom hollered. I was up on my feet again then, and I was bolting to catch up with him.

Then I slipped. I fell onto the tracks. They were trembling violently, Gi. You know how Papa would tell us the story—about how he and his brothers would play on the tracks? And then when the tracks rumbled, their hearts would beat fast in panic because they knew a train was approaching? That's what it was like. And I couldn't get away.

It was like a dream—or rather, a nightmare. I couldn't understand why I was stuck, but I was. And then the train howled again, and I knew I was in the gravest danger I'd been in my whole life. My life flashed before my eyes then.

Then Tom was before me, and his eyes were wide in horror. He grabbed my arms, trying to wrench me off the tracks then. He was hollering some sort of a prayer, I think, but I was in too much of a daze to think clearly.

Will flashed out of the corner of my eye.

I hollered then, I think. I realized a screaming pain tore at my foot.

The next thing I knew, Tom had wrapped his arms tightly around me. I think he was trying to shield me from the oncoming train. Then suddenly the train was tearing by, and we had tumbled on the ground. I felt the hot breath of the beast as it tore by, and I realized I was tumbled on top of both Tom and Will.

Will had managed to yank us to safety.

My shoe was squashed though. The train had swallowed it.

I was so scared, Gi. I think I burst out in a wail when the train had finally passed and then reached out to Tom and Will. They both pulled me into a hug, and we all sat there a long time, very shaken.

Then we stood up. Or, they stood up. I tried to, but I had twisted my ankle again and my toe was bleeding pretty badly. A spike from the tracks had driven through my shoe, which was why I had gotten stuck and which was why my shoe hadn't made it to safety.

Will carried me home. He sorta laughed on the way, saying he'd carried you this way once, only it was to a train station instead of from a train station.

He really misses you, Gi.

Tom came by yesterday. When I mentioned the quarantine to him, he said, "To heck with quarantine." Same as Will.

Doctor Murray thinks things are pretty clear now, anyway. Will and Donny and Mama and Papa and me aren't allowed out of the house, still, but he turned a blind eye to Tom coming to visit me, once again laid up on the sofa.

"How are you?" he asked, a half-smile on his face.

"Not very well," I said, looking up at him with tears in my eyes.

"What's wrong?" he asked in alarm.

"Beth just died!" I burst into tears and buried my face in my pillow. I'm still reading *Little Women*, as you can tell. And I've grown to feel no shame in crying in front of Tom. I've gotten rather used to it.

He didn't laugh at me, but I think he wanted to. Instead, he just patted my head and said, "Do you want me to find a new Beth for you, pet?"

"Stop it," I said, pushing his hand away. But I stopped crying and put the book under the pillow. I sat up, saying, "What do you want?"

"I'm leaving."

"You're what?" It felt like the world droned out then, Gi.

"I'm going to find Mrs. Harvey."

"Oh." I teared up and looked away. "Will you come back?"

"Of course," Tom laughed, turning my chin. "I can't stay away."

"Oh." I looked at him.

His pale blue eyes looked hesitant for a moment, and he said, "I said I've hopped trains before, 'member?"

"Yeah."

"Well, I hopped trains for about six months, trying to get away from the hard life. And come to find out, my grampa was looking for me all that time, trying to find me and give me a new life." He looked at me a moment, thinking. "I want to find Mrs. Harvey. I want to be able to give her a new life too. Grampa said he'll help. I just … I just wanted to tell you. Sometimes if a person keeps running and running, they're keeping themselves from being found and from being given a new life."

"Is that charity?" I asked, rubbing my face with my blanket and looking at him.

"To help someone get back on their feet? No, not really. In that case, it's just a helping hand. Kindness isn't charity, Bess."

"It's awfully confusing the way you put it," I said. "But I think I know what you mean."

Tom's been gone for a day now. Will sat down at the foot of my sofa this morning. His kind dark eyes gazed searchingly into my face, and he said, "I don't need to make Tom run the gauntlet, Bessie. He's a good kid." He paused a moment. "He's a good man."

I smiled then. I couldn't help it. "Yeah," I said.

"And you're a sweet little lady," Will said affectionately, standing up and kissing my hair.

He's a good one, Gi.

Come home, please. Come home to me and Will.

And pray for Tom.

Your sister,

    Bess

May 17th, 1936

Dear Bess,

Oh, my heart! I'm extremely relieved that Donny's going to be well! Give that boy a hug from me! And how jealous I am of your getting to see Will everyday. I am so glad that you approve of him. It would have been dreadful if you didn't. Do Mama and Papa care for him?

Bess! My heart aches for you! How terrible it must have been at Hooverville ... to see a child pass away. My heart twists just thinking about it. You brave soul. I wish I could be as brave as you. I wouldn't have been able to handle myself nearly as courageously as you did. And when you recounted that experience with the train tracks! Are you trying to give me a heart attack? If something would have happened to you ... Oh, Bess! Thank God Will was there!

My, it seems like so much is happening in Kansas. Everyone I care for is there, and I'm all alone in this big city which no longer feels beautiful and cheery.

The boarding house seems so queer lately. The Woods have moved away, and now Karl and his mother are packing up. They're going to live with a relative down south. Karl is quite the little devil, but I think I'll miss his antics. The only familiar face I have to comfort me is Mrs. West.

I'm rather paranoid as of late. Here's why:

I was coming home after a long (and smelly) day of washing dishes. I didn't even want my usual cup of evening tea ... I was exhausted. When I entered my room I got a strange, prickly feeling running up and down my spine. I looked around but didn't see anything that would cause such an odd feeling. I shrugged it away as I sat on the edge of my bed, pried off my shoes, and popped out my earrings. (Even though I wash dishes I can at least look classy while doing so.) I opened my wooden jewelry box to place them alongside my necklace which I keep in there. My heart did one of those uncomfortable leaps as my eyes met an empty box. That necklace that Mama and Papa gave me for my sixteenth birthday was gone. I tried to be reasonable ... I thought that I must have misplaced it. But my room isn't very big, and I don't allow much clutter. I turned the place inside out, but I couldn't find the necklace.

Then, something odd happened the next day. I always close my dresser drawers. I can't stand it if clothes or blankets are busting out of them ... I think it's an eyesore. But the other night my top drawer was a smidgen open. I vividly recall closing it, Bess.

I never locked my door before ... I always felt comfortable and trusting of those in the boarding house. But I'm going to lock it from now on.

– Gi

P.S. I will keep Tom in my prayers. He's a good man, that Tom is. I'm very thankful for that. He will come back for you, Bess. I know he will.

May 22nd, 1936

Dear Gi,

Well, I helped bail Tom out of jail this morning. And Mr. Thomas no longer hates me.

But Will is jabbing my shoulder and insisting I tell you this straight away: "Be careful. And send us a telegram everyday to let us know you're alright." I haven't told Mama and Papa about this, Gi. They've been through enough worry already.

All that to say, Will's insisting this is a very serious situation. In most cases, I would be sounding much more serious about this because it's a very serious matter, and I am concerned about you. But I'm in much too high of spirits to take any situation anything but very lightly at the moment.

I rode a boxcar! Illegally! With old Mr. Thomas! And he lost his umbrella. I hope you have a lot of time on your hands at the moment, for this is going to be a long letter. Know that I have a lot of time to write this because I am bedridden on the sofa. Again. And

Doctor Murray says I shall be laid up much longer this time. Oh, joy.

It was about a week after Tom left to find Mrs. Harvey. I was lying on the sofa because, though I could walk on my foot, Doctor Murray told me not to participate in any strenuous activities, lest I wrench it again. I was coming to the end of *Little Women*. Actually, I had reached the chapter where Amy learns of Beth's death. It was quite the most enthralling part of the story, actually. And I'm beginning to understand why you gloated when I said Tom was Laurie, and I was sorta like Amy. But all that to say, I was deeply engrossed in my book. Papa and Mama had gone to town; Donny was in school; and Will was scouting around for a news story, I think. He said something about the dust bowl to me, but I was reading and didn't really hear him.

There was an urgent knock on the door. I didn't hear it at first. (I was reading, but I've already mentioned that.) But I did hear the door suddenly swing open. Someone hollered, "Hey, Rowland."

My head shot up. I found myself staring and blinking at old Mr. Thomas. He stared and blinked at me. "I'm ... I'm sorry, ma'am," he said respectfully and a little shyly. "I was lookin' for your pa."

"Is something wrong?" I asked, quite surprised. Mr. Thomas never comes over here.

He hesitated. "No, miss," he said after a moment, fingering the umbrella in his hand. "Nothin' wrong."

"Oh," I said. (I didn't believe him, of course. I'm not stupid.) I stood up, laying my book on the sofa. "Papa's in town. May I help you, Mr. Thomas?"

His brows pinched together as he hesitated again. Finally he said, "Here." And handed me a telegram.

I took it uneasily and scanned the words.

GRAMPA. IN JAIL. INDIANAPOLIS. NEED BAIL MONEY. COME IF POSSIBLE. JIMMY.

"Who's Jimmy?" I asked. Then instantly my fingers flew to my lips. "Tom!"

Mr. Thomas nodded gravely. "I don't know what he did, miss, but I'm darn sure he didn't do nothin' too wrong."

He didn't say it quite that nicely, but I don't like to write curse words, so I'm not going to. (Don't worry, *Tom's* not one to curse. Will probably would wash his mouth out with soap and tar if he ever did, anyway.)

"But ... but he's in jail. All alone, Mr. Thomas. Is there anything else it says?" I was beginning to become frantic. I clutched the paper tightly, turning it this way and that, as if there would be more words typed on it. As if there would be some direction on what to do. I looked up at Mr. Thomas, my eyes feeling watery. "What do we do?" I asked.

"Well," Mr. Thomas said, leaning on his umbrella, "I was going to ask your pa for advice. The last passenger train left thirty minutes ago. There ain't nothin' else comin' through today except the 3:45 East. But she's a freighter."

I bit my lip. "East, you say?"

Gi, I proposed the most absurd thing next. And what's more absurd is he thought about it for three seconds and agreed. But train hopping was the only option in my frantic mind just then.

I left a note on the counter. Mr. Thomas signed it as well. (For verification, he said.) I asked him if he thought Mama and Papa would be angry with me. He said no. They'd be angry at him. That didn't quite reassure me, Gi, but it sounded a little better. We took his rickety old Model T down to the railroad tracks. I asked him why we didn't just drive in that. (I began to fear the railroad tracks again, you see, for I had a very bad experience last time I tried to hop a train. If you'll recall.) He said gas was low, and it probably wouldn't take us as far as Indianapolis before it just gave up and died. He said it was likely she would die a very bloody death, and he didn't reckon I would like to see that. To be honest, I didn't know what to say in response to that. I think he was joking.

So we hopped a train. We were going to just climb in a boxcar before the train started moving. Mr. Thomas had heard the whole story of how Tom and I were almost run over a couple weeks ago, and he downright forbid we use Tom's method. But that didn't happen. We reached town just as the train whistle shrieked, and the train was beginning to move. Mr. Thomas slammed on the breaks of the car, and we sprang out.

There wasn't much communication between us. We mutually knew that we needed to get on that train, and we both saw two young boys running along the side of it and swinging up into a boxcar. And we followed them. It was the most terrifying experience ever. All I could think of was Tom and how he wasn't there to help me now and how that was just it—he wasn't there. He was in jail. And I had to help him get out.

So I grabbed the ladder as my feet were pounding, and I was sort of flung onto the train by the speed. Mr. Thomas was right behind me. We sat breathing heavily as the Kansas countryside rolled by, faster and faster, until the world was a blur, and we were really on our way East.

That's when it hit me what I had done. Mama and Papa were going to be worried sick. (This worry and the worry of Donny brought me to the conclusion that I shouldn't tell them about your burglaries. They're rather tuckered out from all their worrying.) I told Mr. Thomas of my fears. He just patted my knee and said, "Well, Miss Rowland, your pa's a good finder. If he's really worried sick, he'll find you, sure as day."

I knitted my eyebrows together. "How do you know Papa is such a good finder?" I asked him, holding tightly to a crate as my hair whipped in my face. The world was going by fast. It was strangely exhilarating.

Mr. Thomas breathed for a few moments, finally saying, "Your pa—when he was a youngster living in your old house—he was quite the mischievous fellow. I lived along 'cross the road then, too. And your pa was always teasin' my daughter mercilessly, taking her hair ribbons and pullin' her braids. He was deeply in love with her."

I blinked. "Pardon?"

"He loved her. My daughter. Hannah."

I was rather shocked. Papa used to love Tom's late mother? It was difficult for me to believe. "What's that got to do with him being a good finder?" I asked after a moment.

Mr. Thomas rubbed his chin. "Well," he said, "one day Hannah just took off. She was always impulsive. Wild. Didn't think I cared for her much, but missie, I tell you the flat truth when I say I loved my little girl more than anything else on this earth. I was worried sick, but your pa ... well, I think he about lost his mind. He went after her. He was flat broke, but he did just what we're doing. He hopped a freighter. His pa came over and told me; I sorta had a heart attack then, for I loved your pa as if he were my own boy.

"He didn't show up again for three weeks. One day I was sitting on my front porch, though, and I looked up. There he was, hunched up and walkin' down the road. Well, I tore down to meet him. 'Where's Hannah?' I asked him. 'Where's my girl?'

"He looked up at me, and I saw a broken heart in his eyes. 'I ... she's alright, mister Thomas.'

"'Where is she?' I growled, grabbing his shoulders and shaking him.

"Your pa scratched his head, his eyes reddening. 'I told her I knew I'd find her. And she said she don't love me, sir. She said so. And I promised not to tell where she is.'

"'Listen to me, boy, and you listen good,' I told him then. 'Tell me where she's at. If she don't love you, why are you so blamed set against going against her ways and telling me?'

"'Because I love her,' your pa said. And ever since that day, we sorta crossed sides. We both loved Hannah, we did. But he wouldn't tell me where she was. Ever since then, we've sorta been set against each other. Even when the spark that drew him to Hannah died, and he fell in love with your ma, we ain't never spoken hardly a word. Sorry if I've ignored you, ma'am, but I wasn't sure what your pa would think if I was kind to you and begrudging to him."

"Why did you come to him now, then?" I asked softly, hugging my chest.

Mr. Thomas didn't say anything for a moment. Finally he looked at me. "Because he's a good finder. And I knew he'd help me find a way to get to Jimmy."

I nodded slowly. "I understand," I said.

The train screamed along the tracks deep into the night. It wasn't until about four o'clock in the morning that we reached Indianapolis. (It was God's working that the train didn't stop until then, Gi. You'll see why soon.)

As we neared the city of Indianapolis, the train suddenly slowed to a halt. It woke me up, but Mr. Thomas was awake already. He was peering out the boxcar into the darkness. Several beams of light began flashing, coming our way.

"What is it?" I asked, rubbing the sleep from my eyes. My back hurt like the dickens. Boxcars are not comfortable places to sleep, Gi.

"I don't know," Mr. Thomas said under his breath. "But I don't think it's good."

Did you know hopping trains is illegal, Gi? We didn't at the time.

The next thing I knew, a rough man had grabbed my arm and wrenched me out of the boxcar. I screamed. It was partially from fear, but it was mostly from the burning pain that suddenly consumed my ankle when I crashed to the ground. I grabbed it, unable to speak for a moment. I looked up as Mr. Thomas was yanked out of the train and thrown next to me.

"Bums!" the man spat at us, kicking my leg. "Git up!"

I tried, but I gasped in pain. "I can't!" I whimpered.

Mr. Thomas dropped his umbrella and stood up. His face was pinched with anger and pain, but he grabbed my arms and helped me to my feet. I ground my teeth together and felt like I might faint from the pain. "Let me talk to them, miss," Mr. Thomas whispered to me. Then he straightened and said, "Excuse me, fellow, but what in God's name are you doing?"

The man raised the butt of his gun—he was carrying a gun, Gi!—and I screamed, "Stop! Who are you?"

Just then several more men with clubs and rifles encircled us. And we were joined by hobos! They must have been on the train as well—actually, I'm certain they were on the train as well. I saw the two young boys who hopped on before us earlier that day.

The man whom I yelled at stepped toward me, snarling, "Don't ye know it's illegal to hop trains, you vermin?"

"No," I protested, "we didn't know!"

He grinned, spitting a stream of tobacco juice at my feet. "Ain't that be a pretty pity?" Then he turned to the rest of them. "Round 'em up! Take 'em to the clink! You gentle people enjoy your stay." He snorted, tipping his hat to us, and swaggered away.

And Mr. Thomas and I and the hobos were marched to jail. It was the most excruciating walk I had ever endured. I swore then that I had broken my ankle—or rather, the man had broken it. But Doctor Murray said it was just another sprain. I'm beginning to despise these things.

The jail was lit up by bright white lights when we reached it. The sheriff took one look at us, rolled his eyes, and beckoned to his deputy. "Split up the genders and keep 'em for awhile."

"'Til when?" the deputy complained. "We already got that other group takin' up the cells, sir. We got no room for these ones."

The sheriff breathed a long sigh that was almost a growl. He ran his hands along his bald head and said, "Let those ones go. The government can't argue with me when I tell 'em I can't lock up close to a hundred bums in our bitty jail."

So the deputy made us wait as he went in and unlocked the cells and filed out the other hobos. As they marched by, some tired-looking, some triumphant-looking, some defiant-looking, I saw a tall redhead and let out a shriek. "Tom!"

I ran toward him and threw my arms around him. He's so much taller than me that I actually sorta pinned his arms to his sides, because I cannot reach his neck very well to give him a proper hug. Anyway, he stood grinning like a fool. Then he bent down and whispered in my ear, "I don't know why, but I knew you'd find me."

I looked at him and gasped. "What happened?" I cried, touching the welt on his freckled cheek.

"Oh, this?" He shrugged. "Bulls."

"Pardon?"

"Railroad bulls. They're hired by the railroad to keep hobos off the freighters. They're a brutal kind. Really brutal." His eyes gleamed, and I could tell he thought very little of them.

I stepped back to tell him that his grampa came, too, when I gasped again. This time from my ankle.

"What's wrong?" Tom asked in alarm.

I lifted my chin. "Bulls." I felt very proud to have experienced the adventurous things he's experienced. Since when did scary excitement make me proud, Gi? What on earth is wrong with me?

Tom's eyes widened. "What do you mean, Hiccup?" (He's called me 'hiccup' on occasion, ever since that time I got the hiccups. It's most exasperating.)

Then I explained what happened, and Mr. Thomas gave Tom a wad of cash. So that Tom could bail *us* out of jail. Turns of events are so amusing.

The sheriff was very kind to us when he found out we had money. I really hope that I never become a person like that. A person who cares more about money than people. It's perfectly disgusting. He offered to have one of his deputies drive us to the train station so that we could catch the next passenger home, but we refused because we don't think much of him at all.

"But your ankle, ma'am," the sheriff said, raising his eyebrows in faux concern.

"No problem," Tom said coolly and picked me up. He carried me all the way to the train station, Gi! He's very strong.

It was as we were walking through the city (it was finally beginning to get light out) that I realized there were four of us walking along instead of three. Mrs. Harvey was trailing behind us! I pointed her out to Tom, and he exclaimed, "Drat!" (*He* doesn't curse. I told you.)

He turned to her, apologizing for forgetting her in the moment, and explained to us how he had found her. They were on their way back to Kansas when the bulls caught them. Tom said the only reason he sent

Mr. Thomas a telegram was because you never know how long they'll keep you. "Sometimes it's only a night," he said. "But once I was in jail for a whole week. It was excruciating. The only thing keeping me alive was when I'd look out the cell window at night and see the—"

"Moon," I finished, a little sleepily. We were on the train at this point. Mrs. Harvey and Mr. Thomas sat across from us. I was sitting by the window. It's so much nicer riding a train with actual seats.

"Yeah," Tom smiled, looking at me. "The moon."

Mama and Papa were mad at me. Papa made Mr. Thomas come into the kitchen, I presume to confront him, while Mama and Mrs. Harvey nursed the wounds the bulls gave me and Tom. I was exhausted by then. And it was only 3:00 in the afternoon. "You know," I said, wincing from my ankle-pain, "I think adventure really isn't my cuppa tea."

"Yeah," Tom said, "I never thought it was." He winked at me.

It's now 5:00. Actually, it's 5:48. My, I've been writing for almost an hour! Anyway, Tom and Mr. Thomas have gone back home. Mrs. Harvey is going to be working for them from now on. She's going to be a live-in maid. I teased Tom and said she's going to be his nanny. He rolled his eyes and said, "I've missed you, too."

Papa and Mr. Thomas must have made up. They no longer aren't speaking to each other anyway. That must be a good sign.

Mama and Papa lectured me, too, by the way. I won't go into that, though.

I need to go now. I'm about to fall asleep even though I'm in strangely high spirits. Will just walked in and said, "Still writing, kiddo?"

"Yeah," I said.

"Tell her I miss her," he said.

He misses you, Gi.

Good night,

    Bess

May 28th, 1936

Bess!

I have never known you to be so adventurous before! How scared you must have been when the bulls caught you! Sometimes I think of riding the rails, but I'm rather clumsy, and I'm afraid I'll get run over by a train, especially after your last terrifying letter. How glad I am that you found Tom! It's extremely witty that you went to bail him out of jail, and he ended up bailing you out!

My! I didn't know that about Papa and Mr. Thomas' daughter. You see? I knew Mr. Thomas didn't hate you.

I received a letter from Will this week. Here's what he said:

> *Dearest Gi,*
>
> *Well, adventure sure runs in your family, though I didn't expect it from Bessie. I suppose she's told you the whole story by now. You Rowlands are an adventurous bunch, aren't*

you? How am I supposed to keep up with you all?

Bessie told me about your break in. Why didn't you include that in your last letter to me? And don't get mad at Bessie for telling me. She's worried about you, and so am I. You're so stubborn. Too stubborn. Be careful, Gi. Lock your doors. Don't go out by yourself after dark, and don't go into Central Park or alley ways. Call me overly protective if you'd like, but I'm worried about you and couldn't stand it if something happened to you. Please, heed my words, would you? And if any young fellows are asking you to go dancing or to Broadway shows with them, I'll wring their necks.

Yours faithfully,
Will

Now Bess, please, please, *please* don't recount this letter I'm writing to anyone. It's going to be the most difficult one I've written yet, and I can't bear to think of Mama, Papa, and Will reading it.

I lost my job. Again. I also lost all my worldly goods. That's why I was in Central Park. Yes, I went into Central Park. Yes, I know I promised Will that I wouldn't. Yes, I broke my promise like the silly goose

I am. I'm sure you're confused, so let me start at the beginning.

I arrived at the seafood restaurant three minutes late the other day. That's why I thought Mr. Opal wanted to see me: to scold me for being late. It wasn't. He told me that I would no longer be working at *Opal's Fine Seafood*. He said that he couldn't afford to pay me anymore. I begged him, telling him how desperately I need this job to help my family in Kansas. He said he sympathizes, but he's got a family that he has to take care of too. So I left, resolving to think over my situation at the boarding house and then search for another job.

When I got home, Mrs. West was in a panic! She met me at the door, her face stricken pale.

"What's wrong?" I asked, grabbing her hand.

"They're gone!"

"Who's gone?"

"Those new boarders! They just ransacked the place and left! Check your room, Miss Rowland, and pray that everything is still there!"

I ripped off my hat and threw it on the chair in the parlor before hoofing it upstairs. I tore down the hallway, then stopped short. My bedroom door was wide open. My bed was stripped down. All the blankets and the pillow were missing. My books that I keep on my desk were gone, along with my typewriter. All the drawers to my dresser were flung open and completely emptied. My breath caught inside me as I hurried to check under my bed for my savings box. A lump formed in my throat when I found only dust. Everything was gone, Bess. Everything I own except for the clothes I was wearing and the purse in my hands. Everything else had disappeared, as if it had never been there at all. I was in shock for a long moment. Then I heard Mrs. West's footsteps come behind me. She placed a gentle hand on my shoulder.

"Oh, Miss Rowland! I can't express how deeply sorry I am for this!" Her voice was broken.

"What happened, Mrs. West? Did you see them leave? What were their names?"

"I had just informed them that their rent was overdue when they came down for breakfast. They must have had this all planned out ... what time you would be at work ... knowing that I can't hear anything when I'm washing dishes and singing along to the radio. They ransacked all the rooms, then hightailed it out of here fast as a jack rabbit. Miss Rowland, I am so sorry!" Tears ran down her wrinkled cheeks. "And I have their names, but I'm sure they're not their real ones and likely won't get us anywhere."

I took a deep breath as I beheld my bare room. I am a victim to a robbery, Bess. It's such a helpless feeling. I would have been able to deal with it better if I had coffee.

"Where do you think they went?" I asked through gritted teeth.

Mrs. West shrugged. "I ... " Then her face changed. "Oh my, I think I know where they were going!"

I turned. "Where?"

"I overheard them talking last night about a man named Charlie that they needed to meet in the Hooverville—the Central Park Hooverville. That was before I found out they were thieves, of course, so I paid it no mind."

"Have you called the police?"

"Of course I did, dear. But they said it was probably a hopeless case. There are too many robberies these days. It's scandalous."

"Well, then. I suppose I'll have to find them myself, won't I?" I said, turning on my heel and tearing down the stairs.

Mrs. West was right behind me. "What? Are you daft?"

"No. I just want my savings back. I need that money, Mrs. West."

"But ... but Central Park? A young lady like you? There are ... there are dark characters in there, Miss Rowland! It's not safe to walk in there alone. Never has been and never will!"

"There are nice characters, too. Don't forget the nice ones. I'll be fine."

"Oh, my. If Mr. Reeves were here he'd—"

"Well, he's not here, is he?" I snapped at her, tears burning in my eyes. I immediately felt horrid. "I'm sorry, Mrs. West. Excuse me."

I threw open the door and hurried down the street. I went to get coffee first, certain that I could handle anything once it was in my system. I was desperate for it. But then I remembered that I couldn't afford it. Now that was a horrible feeling: to realize I didn't have enough money for coffee! I blame what happened next on the lack of caffeine.

I couldn't understand why Will wouldn't want me to go into Central Park. For heavens sake, you've been to a Hooverville a few times, and you were perfectly safe! It was broad daylight, I was angry, and I didn't have coffee, which would have made me more ... *cordial*. No one would challenge me.

What met my eyes as I entered Central Park was heart wrenching. Shacks by the dozen were set up, small fires blazing outside them. Women huddled around, cooking whatever they could over it. Little children played in the dirt. Men were dressed in rags. I walked up and down the rows, my heart splitting at the sight of every person my eyes met. I offered smiles to them, which they gave me in return. I wish I had something for them, but all I had to live on was in my purse. I sadly couldn't spare anything. Not even for coffee. I was on the lookout for those three boarders, and I was sure I'd be able to spot them right away. They had a very distinct look about them.

I hoped I hadn't missed them.

After an agonizing hour in heels, my marching turned to shuffling. I slowed down as I turned down a curve in the pathway and entered a wooded area thick with brush. I realized I was leaving the Hooverville, so I stopped for a moment and caught my breath before turning around again.

I shouldn't have stopped, Bess. I should have continued walking.

My skin grew clammy as I heard footsteps crunch the gravel behind me. I whipped around, now facing two young, burly men. My heart dropped to the pit of my stomach.

"What's a nice lady like you doing in the heart of Central Park?" the blond haired one asked, inching closer with a smirk on his face. (I'll just give them names so I don't confuse you. Blond hair is Fred, brown hair is Harry.)

I took a step backward, hardly able to speak. "I ... uh ... I don't suppose you've seen two men, one bald and one with a mustache? Or a woman with unusually long fingernails around, have you?"

"Can't say as I have," Fred said, almost politely. He hardly looked older than your Tom.

"Just hand over the purse," Harry growled. Then he gave Fred a shove. "Don't chat with her, idiot."

I gripped my purse tighter, lifting my chin. "I will not. Please, leave me alone. I have urgent business to attend to."

"What did you say to me?" Harry drew nearer to me, his dark eyes piercing.

I know the safe thing to have done would have been to hand over the purse and be on my way, but I needed my purse. I needed that money, Bess! And I grew angry.

"I will not hand over my purse." I turned, but two hands grabbed my arms and wrenched them behind my back. A shot of pain traveled up and down my arm, and I screamed.

"Make her shut up!" Harry hissed at Fred.

Fred clamped his hand over my mouth and whispered, "Please shut up."

I screamed even louder.

"I said make her shut up!" Harry snapped.

"I'm tryin'!" Fred clamped his hand tighter on my mouth. I tried screaming. I kicked. I finally bit his hand, and he jumped back. "She bit me!" he yelled.

My purse was yanked off my arm, then Harry gave me a shove to the ground. "Thanks a lot for the purse, lady." Then he and Fred sneaked off into the dark woods.

I picked myself up, clutching my pained arm. A bruise was already starting to appear. I stumbled back toward the Hooverville and a middle-aged woman spotted me. She flew to my side in an instant, her children trailing behind.

"Miss, are you all right?"

That's when I realized I had a large, bloody gash on the side of my face.

"Someone just stole my purse!" My voice was strained.

"Come, let me clean that cut for you," she said kindly.

I sat on a wooden stool outside her shack as she placed a cold, damp cloth to the side of my face. Her children, three boys and two girls, sat on the grass and watched me.

I told Mrs. West that there were nice people in Central Park. I was right. This woman even gave me a bowl of soup and insisted that I eat it. It touched me that she would share her food with me—a stranger—when there was only a meager amount.

I thanked her, wishing I could give them something in return, then headed home.

Tears sprang to my eyes as I realized what this meant. Bess, I have nothing. Well, that's not entirely true. I had just purchased stamps yesterday and forgot that I still had them in my sweater pocket. At least I can still write!

Mrs. West is very sweet and merciful and is allowing me to stay even though I'm completely broke, so continue writing to this address for now. Please, don't tell Mama and Papa or Will. They would be terribly worried, and I am determined to make it through this on my own.

Take care of yourself, Bess. And tell Will that I can't afford to send a telegram everyday.

– Gi

June 2nd, 1936

Georgiana Rowland,

You're a fool. And I'm more of a fool than you. I didn't tell anyone of what you did. I know I should. I know I need to. But there's that distinct sisterly understanding in me that won't allow it. You sure make my life tough to live. Every morning I've woken up feeling guilty and fearful.

Enough of that, though. I've sent you two dollars. It was in my savings, but you need it more than any of us right now, so here it is. Please don't be foolish and buy coffee with it.

Papa took me to town the other day and bought me a peppermint stick. Remember how he would do that when we were little girls? I felt like a little girl again. "C'mon, Bess," he said that morning, "I'm goin' to get some flour, and I want you to come."

I said, "Okay." Ain't nobody gonna cross Papa. Except you.

We strolled to town in silence. My ankle was doing fairly at this point. I couldn't walk very fast, and I sort of hobbled. But I went to town alright. And Doctor Murray said that clearly I'm unable to keep off my feet for long, so I might as well do as I please. I just need to be careful and not go far or walk fast or strain it in any way.

Papa bought the flour from Mr. Yale, and then he told me to pick out a peppermint stick. I kinda blushed and did. I don't know why I got so embarrassed. I wanted a peppermint stick, for sure. I think I just suddenly had one of those moments where I didn't feel myself at all, and instead was no one and was looking at myself as an outsider. Those moments are horrid. And I felt like I was looking at a child, which made me wonder what other people look at me as, and that was a dirty thought. Then I remembered Papa, and we bought the peppermint and went out the door.

We headed back home. It was a hot day out. I think summer's finally settling in. It always settles in Kansas early—before it should logically be summertime. My overalls were beginning to stick to my back, right through my blouse and all.

"Let's stop and rest a bit," Papa said, so we plopped in the tall, rough grasses, and Papa tugged a stem and chewed on it.

I sucked on my peppermint stick. "Papa," I said after a moment, "did you like Hannah Thomas?"

His eyes darted to me. I can never tell what he's thinking. After a moment, he gazed out on the dirt road. "Reckon I did, Bess."

I half-smiled. "You did, Papa."

He looked at me sharply. Then he nodded. "Yeah. I did."

"What was she like?"

"She was a red-head if I ever saw one. And wild. Clumsy. Not a tomboy, not a priss. Just a simple girl who loved life and loved to live it carefree." Papa paused, tearing the dry stem from his lips. "I wanted to be like that."

I frowned in thought, finally biting off a piece of peppermint and chewing it. "Did you love her?"

Papa froze. "I reckon I did."

I took the peppermint from my mouth and licked my lips. I looked at him. "Then how come it didn't work out? If you love someone ... how do you know you truly love them? How do you know it's right?"

His bushy eyebrows knitted together. The shadows of the grasses played games on his face, painting different emotions that I fancied were the hauntings of past feelings. I was confused. And somehow Tom kept demanding my thought's attention at the same moment.

"Love ain't a feeling, Bess. It's a choice. Sure, there will be feelings. But love—if you mean the marriage kind—is both the feeling and the choice. And it's a two-sided deal. I felt and chose Hannah; she didn't feel and choose me. I reckon God didn't mean it to be."

"How did Mama come into all of this?"

A smile flickered across Papa's stubbly jaw. "There was a dance in town here," he said, waving his arm toward the road. "Elizabeth Donovan was a prissy young lady from Chicago. I was the ol' country fellow who was born and raised in Kansas. It was sorta on accident that we danced. I stepped on her toes, and she unashamedly made faces the entire time. I reckon it was love at first dance."

I was terribly confused at this point. There was no coherency to this conversation. I sat up straight, throwing the rest of the peppermint in the grass. "Yes, but Papa," I said restlessly, "how'd you let Hannah go so easily? How come it wasn't true love? Is there more than one true love?"

Papa looked at me a moment, his arm dangling over his knee. "I didn't let Hannah go, Bess. She went. And she weren't mine to begin with. I fancied I loved her, and maybe I did. But the only kind of love-choice I could make was that of a friend. I couldn't choose to love her as a bride because she wouldn't choose to love me as a groom. So the spark faded, and the love as a friend lived on. But friends leave, and she did. So eventually the hours I thought of her passed and were replaced with hours to be lived thriving on other loves. Loves for friends, brothers, sisters, beauty, gladness. Love for a Savior whose love is bigger than anythin'. And eventually He led me to your mama. And I'm right glad He did."

I stared at him, feeling like that was the deepest thing Papa had said to me outside of explaining the Scriptures and telling me about Jesus and the apostles. "Oh," I said. I was quiet for a moment, and then I picked a buttercup next to me. I held it up to my chin, "Do I like butter, Papa?"

He grinned. "Yeah." He picked one and held it up to his chin. "Do I?"

"Yeah," I said, smiling. "Can we have some for supper?"

"'Fraid not," he said, standing up slowly. "Ain't got the milk or money, sugar."

"Drat," I said. "I suppose potatoes and bread will do."

I'm not sure why I recounted all this to you, Gi. I think it's just because I want to keep it all as a memory for me. Maybe I'll copy all this down on separate paper for my own.

Be careful, Georgiana Alexandria Rowland. I mean it. Don't go looking for those thieves. Leave that to the police.

I'm this close to telling Will about the whole matter.

With much, much love and many, many tight hugs,

    Bess

June 9th, 1936

Dear Bess,

Thank you so much for the money! But I feel horrible taking it. After all, I'm in NYC to send money home to you! Things didn't go quite as planned, I'm afraid. And thank you for keeping my last letter a secret ... but next time please don't leave it in plain sight, dear.

Here's my latest letter from Will:

Gi, (Not even dear or dearest ... that's how mad he was.)

I can't believe you. I really can't. You were planning on keeping the boarding house robbery and Central Park ordeal a secret from me? Don't go blaming Bessie. She didn't tell me. I've been taking meals with your family after work, and I came home a little earlier than usual. The house was quiet, and I didn't see anyone about. I sat at the kitchen table, about to go over my notes from that day's interview. That's when I saw a letter lying on the table. I wasn't going to read it, but as I glanced at it, my eyes fell on my name. I see that you didn't want me or your parents to know about your letter. I'm not ashamed that I read something that wasn't mine, Gi. Not this time. I think God laid it there for me to read just so I could talk some sense into your stubborn, beautiful head.

You broke your promise to me, Gi. I vividly recall looking into your eyes and telling you not to go into Central Park by yourself. You promised. You, Georgiana Rowland, promised! Why did you think it was a good idea to hunt the thieves down by yourself? What were you planning on doing if you found them? I know you're trying to be independent and all, but you seem to have twisted the meaning of the word. Being independent doesn't mean keeping secrets from those who care about you. And you must know that I care about you, Gi. It's not a sign of weakness to ask for help. It's humility.

Good Lord, I couldn't control myself when I had finished reading your letter. I was a hot headed mess, ready to whip the stuffing out of everyone and anyone who ever hurt you. I was running a hand through my hair and sputtering when Bessie and Tom walked in. I think Bessie was a little frightened of me. I was shouting. At you. At the thieves. At the blasted distance between Kansas and New York. Tom said something about calming down, and I finally did. I told Bessie that I had read the letter. At first she turned pale, but then a relieved look crossed her face. I think she was thankful not to keep this secret any longer.

Georgiana Alexandria Rowland, when are you going to get off your high horse and ask someone for help? I can't wait for a response to that question. It would take too long. That's why I'm coming back to New York, Gi. I'll be on the 6:45am train on Monday. Please meet me there.

Yours,

    Will

Bess! He's coming back to New York City? You must stop him! It's not that I don't want to see him, because I desperately do, but I need to gather my life together first.

Mrs. West is a dear and cleaned me up after the robbery. She let me wear a pair of her cotton pajamas that evening. I was starting to feel better about life as I sat before the fireplace, and Mrs. West made me a cup of coffee. Bless that lady for knowing I wasn't in the mood for tea ... only strong, black coffee. I was lost in thought as I sat there, thinking what a stupid idea it was to come to NYC. I thought it would be glamorous, but now I realize I was kidding myself. What's glamorous about being robbed, mugged, and jobless? Nothing.

I sat with my legs tucked under me, curled up in a ball on the sofa, and wishing I was home. Wishing Mama was stroking my hair and telling me that everything would be all right. Wishing Papa was smoking his pipe and reading the paper across from me. Wishing you and Donny were telling me stories and making me laugh. Wishing that I was holding Will's hands as he told me how stubborn I was, instead of reading it on paper.

I was a wreck, Bess. I was crying as I drank my coffee. I was pouting like a two-year-old. Then Mrs. West took a seat across from me, nervously smoothing the wrinkles out of her dress.

"It's kind of you to allow me to stay until I get on my feet again," I told her.

"Yes ... um ... Miss Rowland, I need to talk to you about that," she said.

"Oh?" I sat up, wiping my face with the back of my sleeve.

"Yes, well, I ... " She paused, looked at me, then started again. "I lost a good sum of money and possessions in that robbery. Nearly all my money was stolen, Miss Rowland. I can't afford to run this boarding house any longer. You understand, don't you?"

My heart sank to the pit of my stomach. "Oh, of course I understand, Mrs. West."

She looked relieved. "I will continue to give you meals until I close if you'll help me pack up, dear."

I nodded. "All right."

She hesitated for a moment, then said, "Don't you think you should catch a train home to Kansas soon, Miss Rowland?"

I looked down at my hands and studied them as if they were the most interesting things in the world. "I'd be mortified to go home like this. A failure."

"You're hardly a failure, Miss Rowland! These times are hard on everyone," she said, smiling at me, motherly-like.

"Thank you, Mrs. West. But I feel like one. I shouldn't have come. I should have stayed in Kansas."

"Then you wouldn't have met Mr. Reeves."

My eyes shot up, locking with hers. "What does Will have to do with this?"

"Oh, everything. I saw the way he looked at you all those months he lived in New York. You were too blind to see it, Miss Rowland. Every meal he had with you, he was staring at you with such love that I was sure you must have felt it. But you never looked up. And every evening in the parlor ... didn't you ever wonder why he was on the same page of *Oliver Twist* for four months? I wasn't supposed to say anything, but he skipped numerous meals so that he could buy you coffee, take you dancing, and purchase Broadway tickets. The poor man must have lost upward of ten pounds."

My heart was beating fast. "I know that he cares about me but—"

"He loves you, Miss Rowland."

My skin went cold for a moment. Love? Do you really suppose Will *loves* me, Bess? I haven't dared entertain the thought, for I would be heartbroken if all my dreams came crashing down around me once again.

"And I love him," I said softly, surprised to hear my own words. Of course, I've always known I loved him, but I've never said it before!

"Then why on earth are you here and not home with your family and Mr. Reeves?"

"They would be so disappointed in me! I came here to help them, and in order for me to come home, they'd have to send me more money. I'd be the laughing stock of Kansas. *'Gi Rowland takes New York City! Ends up Being Robbed, Jobless, and Can't Even Afford Coffee!'* Oh, it would be humiliating!"

"Well, I can't convince you one way or another, so I'll just head up to bed. But I suggest you think it over. We'll have eggs in the morning, then we'll begin packing, Miss Rowland."

I said goodnight and brooded all night long.

I lost my home this week, Bess. The boarding house has been packed away, and Mrs. West moved in with her sister. That's left me with nowhere to stay, no money, and no job.

So that's why I now reside at the homeless shelter.

No, I am not exaggerating. I sleep on a rickety cot and sleep under a scratchy brown blanket. My pillow is stuffed with rags, so it's a lumpy mess which never feels comfortable from any angle. It's noisy here and *horribly* crowded. It's rather a good thing that I don't have any belongings. Belongings are stolen regularly. I've been taking my meals at the soup kitchen. Bess! I never in all my dreams imagined my life in NYC could end like this! But I am determined to fight my way through this. Don't you dare tell Papa to send money. I came to NYC to work and send the family money, not the other way around.

And then I was violently sick this week. A fever, stomach pains, the chills ... I'm still not feeling well and have spent entire days in bed. I haven't gotten much sleep though, for everyone is talking, and people are constantly in and out. I don't even want coffee. You know I'm ill when I don't want coffee, Bess. If Will comes now, he'll find a bedridden girl who hasn't had a change of clothes in a week.

Please, try to keep Will there. Don't let him come yet. I can't bear the thought of looking the way I do if he comes. I don't want him to see me like this, Bess. I need to get on my feet again. I can do it, so don't worry about me.

– Gi

P.S. Your recount of spending the afternoon with Papa was very sweet, Bess. You and Papa always got along. Whenever I tried having conversations with him, it always ended up with him saying, "What on earth am I going to do with you, Gi Rowland?" I do miss him though.

June 14th, 1936

Dear Gi,

I'm glad Will found that letter.

Tom and I had gone for a walk. He'd said he wanted to show me something. I didn't quite understand the butterflies in my stomach when he said that, but I trusted my heart and expected something wonderful.

We strolled down the road a piece, heading west like we had when Donny and him and I had gotten lost. It was a beautiful day. Warm, but beautiful. The sun beat down upon us, but the warm breezes that blew made up for it. I did nothing with my hair that day, so it blew around my face wildly. I rather liked it.

"You're not going to get us lost again, are you?" I asked Tom with a laugh, as he steered me off the road onto the big, wide, beautiful prairie. There was nothing to see but rolling grasses and blue sky. I thrive off views like that.

"Excuse me?" Tom exclaimed. "I believe it was you who had gotten us lost, mademoiselle. Me? I never get lost."

"Cocky laddie." I shook my head at him with a sly grin. "I recall you seemed pretty lost then."

"Well, yeah." He winked at me. "But you were the one who got us lost. I didn't get us lost."

"Oh, whatever you say." I laughed and ran on ahead of him, breathing in the wanderlust. It struck me deep then, and if Tom had suggested we fly to the moon, I think I would have. He didn't, however. Which was probably good.

Suddenly he was running on ahead of me, and I called, "What was it you wanted to show me?"

"This way!" he shouted, his red hair looking golden in the vivid sunlight.

I strove to keep up with him, but his legs are longer than mine. So he ran up a sudden, unexpected grassy hill before me, and I struggled up after him. He stood at the top, his arms crossed over his chest, and a very pleased look on his face. "What is it?" I gasped, rather out of breath.

His eyes twinkled, and he reached out a hand to help me up. "This."

I gaped. Below us lay a canvas of wildflowers. White ones. Yellow ones. Little blue ones. If I knew more about botany, I'd tell you their names. They were simply beautiful. And there was an ocean of them in that little trench of earth. "I haven't seen flowers like this since before the dust bowl," I breathed, feeling like I might cry from the beauty. Have you ever felt like that? Have you ever wanted to not only enjoy the beauty, but become the beauty and let it consume your thoughts and emotions? I'm so happy that our Creator loves beautiful things.

"Like it?" Tom asked me, touching my hand. "I thought it was pretty. I thought you'd like it."

"I love it," I whispered, squeezing his fingertips. Then I ran down the hillside and sat down right in the midst of the flowers. I laughed. Then I looked up at Tom. His arms were crossed over his chest again, and he wasn't really laughing. He was just staring. I wondered why. "Come on!" I beckoned. "Let's make ropes of them and decorate my house!"

He grinned, lingered on the hilltop a moment longer, and then tramped down and sat down next to me, crushing a couple pretty flowers. I didn't mind. There were hundreds more.

We strung together dozens of the little beauties, and Tom made me a crown for my hair. I made him a necklace of the little blue ones, but he said it would look better on me than him. So he hung it around my neck instead. I was going to make a long chain to wrap around the front porch, but Tom pointed out that it might die on the way home, and it'd be best to enjoy it here anyway. I saw his reasoning.

After awhile, the sun began to beat down upon us harder than before, and we realized we were desperately thirsty. "'Fraid we ought to go, Hiccup," Tom said.

"Yeah, I suppose," I said, looking around me at the flowers. I noticed many were fading from the heat, and I wished it would rain so they could live longer. "Can we come back tomorrow?" I asked. "I want to live amongst them as long as I possibly can."

Tom grinned, standing up. "Sure," he said, holding out his hand. "We can come until the last one shrivels away."

"Don't say that," I said, taking his hand as he helped me to my feet. "I don't like to think of death until it happens. It spoils the here and now."

"True," he replied. "However, knowing that something doesn't last forever reminds you to take nothing for granted."

I saw his reasoning.

We headed back home, and fortunately the warm breezes kept us from drying up in the sun completely. My hair was a wild mess by the time we reached home, but Tom's crown made up for the messiness. It was crafted of the delicate white flowers, and I thought they were very pretty.

We heard shouting as we climbed the front porch. Tom and I looked at one another in alarm, then sprinted into the kitchen. That's when we found Will pacing the floor, running his hands through his hair and shouting into space.

I was a little scared. I'd never once heard Will raise his voice or look so angry.

"How could you?" he bellowed, taking a step toward me.

I shrank back, grabbing Tom's arm. "What did I do?" I asked shakily.

Will flung his hands in the air and stalked toward the sink, his jaw clenched. "Thieves!" he exclaimed. "Thieves, and she didn't tell me!"

I think my mind was frozen at this point, because I still didn't understand what he was talking about. Tom took a step toward Will and said, "Look, pal, calm down, and tell us what's wrong."

Finally Will sat down at the kitchen table. He ran his hands over his face a moment before handing me a piece of paper. I took it with trembling hands and then dropped it on the table again, covering my mouth with my fingers. It was your letter.

At first I was horrified, but then all of a sudden relief washed over me and tears sprang to my eyes. "I didn't know what to do," I whispered.

Will suddenly erupted from his seat, and I recoiled, afraid he was angry with me for not telling him. Tom stepped in front of me, saying soothingly, "Come on, take it easy, Reeves."

The fire in Will's eyes suddenly cooled. "I'm sorry, Bessie," he said gently. "I'm not angry at you. I'm upset with Gi. I could kill those dirts who hurt her. I could kill the blasted distance between Kansas and New York!" His voice was rising again, and I edged closer to Tom.

"God, I love her," Will said suddenly.

I looked up.

He was staring at me intensely. "I'm headin' back to New York," he said, abruptly quitting the room.

Tom and I looked at one another. "Men are so strange," I mused, sitting down at the kitchen table and taking a deep breath.

"No," Tom said, sitting down next to me. "Women are strange."

Will didn't tell Mama and Papa the real reason he was leaving. "Gotta take care of something," was all he told them. I don't know if it was wise of him, but I knew I didn't want to worry them about you. I knew telling them would ruin your pride, and I knew the only person who ought to ruin your pride should be you yourself.

Besides, Will's coming to protect you. I know you'll be alright.

He left yesterday, Gi. I suppose he's there now. I can't stop him now, you know. I wouldn't stop him anyway, even if I could. Like Will told you, you have a warped idea of independence. It's time you understand what independence is, and it's time you understand that everyone needs help these days. Even you. And it's okay to ask for help.

Yours,

Bess

June 29th, 1936

Gi,

Where are you? It's been two weeks since I last heard from you, and I was certain you'd have sent me a reassurance of your safety and Will's arrival before now. I was certain that, even if you were too angry at me to write, *he* would have at least sent me something!

I'll try not to worry. I haven't told Mama or Papa anything about this, but I'm worried. Tom's my chief confidant on this matter.

He came over for breakfast this morning. He'd told Mama he'd provide maple syrup if she'd make pancakes. And she agreed.

They were sizzling on the stove when he pounded up the front steps and burst in through the screen door. He has a distinct slam indicating his arrival. I was sitting at the kitchen table, and Donny was sitting under the kitchen table, trying to make Priss growl like a lion. (He still hasn't forgotten how that cat is supposed to be a lion to guard me at night.)

"Sir James has arrived," Tom declared, tossing the bottle of maple syrup through the air, catching it with his left hand and sliding it across the table to me. "We can eat now."

I laughed, grabbing it just as it started to slide off the table, and Mama said, "I'm sorry, son, but they aren't ready yet. Go fetch some eggs, if you want them with your hot cakes."

"Yes, ma'am." Tom saluted and vanished.

I bit my lip and followed him out to the chicken coop. "Tom," I said, swinging into step beside him, "I'm worried."

"'Bout what?" he asked, turning. He leaned against the doorway of the coop, crossing his arms.

"About Will and Gi."

"What's wrong with 'em?"

"Nothing," I said, rubbing my lips. "I haven't heard a word from Gi in two weeks. I've gone no longer than one week without hearing from her." I paused, shivering. "What if something happened to them? How come she hasn't sent word?"

Tom looked grave. "I'm sorry, Bess."

"Don't say that!" I cried.

He looked confused. "I didn't mean anything by—"

"You sound like you think something awful has happened to them!" I fought back tears.

Tom straightened, lifting his eyebrows. "I didn't mean that at all, Bessie."

"Don't call me that, either," I said, frowning. "That's Will's pet name for me."

Tom sighed. "I'm just trying to sympathize."

He wasn't doing a very good job of it. I bit my lip and leaned against the coop next to him. "What do you think is wrong?" I whispered, looking up at him.

He hesitated. "Maybe the letter got lost in the mail."

"Maybe." I wasn't convinced, though, and my worry was growing by the minute.

"Look, Bess," Tom said in exasperation. "Stop worrying. I don't like to see you like this. Leave the worrying to me, okay? I'll worry for you."

"Yeah," I said. "Okay."

I've been trying not to worry. For example, I've been trying to think about the Independence Day picnic coming up in a few days. Mama's making me a new dress. We went to town last week, and she let me pick out a feed sack for a new dress. I was originally planning on a red gingham or yellow paisley because red and yellow are all I tend to wear.

However, as I was digging through the pile of feed sacks in Mr. Yale's store, I stumbled across a print I fell in love with. Sprigs of white flowers dotted the pale pink material, and I hesitated only a moment before asking Mama if she thought I would look alright in it. She smiled. "I think it's perfect. Pink will complement your complexion very well."

You and Mama always have such good taste in style.

Oh, Gi, please write soon.

Tom's reading over my shoulder now. He nudged me and said I was supposed to leave the worrying to him. I'm afraid I'm not able to do that.

I wonder if I should tell Mama and Papa.

Write soon, Gi. I'm serious.

Love,

Bess

July 2nd, 1936

Bess,

Please forgive me for not writing sooner! These last two weeks have been a complete whirlwind. I have so much to write. I don't know where to start. I just had five cups of coffee, so I'm writing at a furious speed, and I can't sit still.

Monday crept up on me too soon. I was so sick that time meshed all together. Days and nights flew by without my noticing or caring. I was curled up on my cot and sweating from a lingering fever when I remembered Will's letter.

"What day is it?" I asked the woman on the next cot over.

"Monday," she said gruffly, obviously not wanting to talk. She was smoking right toward me. I coughed and sat up on my elbow.

"What time is it?" My eyes darted all over the shelter for a clock.

"How am I supposed to know?" She puffed another cloud of smoke.

I ran a hand through my hair, but my fingers got snagged in a knot. I hadn't brushed it in a week. The room spun around me, and I felt the blood drain from my head. I laid my head back down for a moment.

"It's nearly eight," a young woman across from me said.

"Eight?" I sat up quickly again, regretting it immediately. I felt like I was on that carousel at the state fair, and I couldn't get off.

"Lady, you better take it easy," the woman said. "You don't look so good."

"No, I have to get up." I swung my legs off the cot, and they touched the cold, hardwood floor.

"Got somewhere to go?" she asked.

"I have to get to the train station," I said, searching under my cot for my shoes and praying no one stole them.

"Gonna ride the rails?"

"No!" I found my shoes and slipped them on. "I was supposed to meet someone there at 6:45!" I wanted to cry, Bess. I wanted to be with Will right at that moment, but at the same time I didn't. You don't know how horrible I looked. I was sure he'd be repulsed by my appearance.

"Does this person know where you're livin'? Maybe they'll come here."

"No." I nervously tried brushing through my hair with my fingers. "I'll have to go find him."

I left the shelter with wobbly legs. My mind was whirling. The first thing I needed to do was clean myself up. But where? I headed toward Mrs. West's boarding house thinking that perhaps I could sneak in through a window ... and hope that her water was still on. I kept my head low and my gait swift as I pushed through the throngs of people. I could see the boarded up house ahead and thoughts of water and soap happily danced in my head. That's when my eyes fell on someone standing on the boarding house steps.

Will.

Our eyes locked. Time stood still. Then suddenly he bounded down the steps and started running toward me. Bess, I was so overwrought with emotions that I let out a scream and ran the other way. I didn't want him to see me like this! I heard him shout, "Gi!" But I kept running, not sure what in the world I was doing. I think I was suffering from delirium. I popped into the first establishment I could find. It was a bookstore.

I hurried down the aisle lined with beautiful books. I would have stopped to admire them if I wasn't so scared of Will finding me. I hid behind a ladder and ran my fingers along the spines of the books. My head was spinning. I thought I was going to faint, so I sat down and leaned my back against the bookshelf. I heard the door creak open. I held my breath and closed my eyes. Spots danced in front of my eyes, and the fever chills were back.

I heard footsteps, starting out faint, and then growing louder. I slowly opened my eyes. Will was kneeling in front of me. His eyes studied my face. "Gi," he said softly.

Then I started crying. Bawling. Sobbing.

He reached out a hand and touched the side of my face gently. "Everything's going to be okay."

I leaned forward and wrapped my arms around his neck, still crying like a baby. I'm sure I was a sight, but for a moment I didn't care. I soaked Will's sleeve in tears and felt safe in his arms. He stroked my hair as best he could. (It was a rat's nest.)

"Hey. You people planning on buying a book? If not, get out."

I looked up and noticed a short man with a bald head standing in front of us. I wiped away the tears with the back of my hand.

Will stood up, reached out his hands to me and pulled me to my feet. "Yes, can we please have a copy of *Little Women?*" he said.

As the owner went to find a copy of the book, I peered at Will with a curious expression.

"I heard you Rowland girls like that book," he said with a grin. He purchased it and then stuck the book in his satchel. He wrapped an arm around me as we left the bookstore. I was feeling weak, so I clung to his arm to keep my knees from buckling.

"There's a boarding house not far from here. I got a room for you," he said. Then he glanced at me. "Should I get the doctor?"

"No," I said. "I'll be all right."

"Want some coffee?"

"No."

He stopped walking and stared at me. "Oh, heaven help us, you really are sick!"

"Don't look at me!" I said, staring at the ground.

"Why?"

I could feel his stare. "I'm an ugly mess!"

"What?"

I glanced up. He was looking at me. He seemed genuinely confused by my words.

"I haven't washed in over a week, my hair is a mess, I smell, I—"

"Georgiana Rowland, is that why you ran away from me?"

I nodded.

He laughed!

"What?" I slapped his arm.

"Gi, you're the prettiest girl I ever met. I mean it."

Well, that was the last thing in the world I expected to hear while appearing like I lived in the dump all my life.

"Oh … thanks."

"You're welcome."

When we arrived at the boarding house, I was feeling sick to my stomach. The landlady showed me to my room, and there I stayed until noon the next day. I was provided with a wash tub and a new dress. I will never take baths for granted ever again! It was the most wonderful feeling in the world to have my hair washed and smelling decent once again.

I finally emerged from my room and headed downstairs. The smell of coffee made me giddy. Will was sitting at the dining room table, but there wasn't any food in front of him. Either he had already eaten, or he was skipping meals to save money. I felt ashamed when I thought of how much money he must have dished out to come here and pay for room and board. He doesn't have much money, but he's very generous with it.

"Good morning," I said.

"Good afternoon." He smirked.

I laughed as I sank into a chair next to him. "I guess I overslept, didn't I?"

"A little. Are you feeling better?"

"Coffee sounds heavenly right now."

"Good. That must mean you're feeling better." He grabbed the coffee pot and poured me a large mugful. I took it gratefully, downing half of it within a minute. Then the landlady brought me a bowl of hot porridge, leaving us to a silent room.

Finally Will said, "Gi, we need to talk."

"Yes, I suppose we do."

"What are your plans now that you don't have a job or a place to stay on your own?" he asked.

I took a long sip of coffee, then looked at him. "Will, I ... I want to go home." My voice buckled. "I'm so tired of trying to survive here. I'm so tired of trying to prove my independence to everyone. I didn't want to give up, but I can't do this any longer."

Will was smiling at me. "Good. Because I already purchased two train tickets for Kansas."

"What?" I gaped at him.

"I'm taking you home, Gi."

"But ... but Will, you don't have the money—"

"I know what I'm doing, Gi. I know what I need to do. I need to take you home."

Home. What a beautiful word that is, Bess!

"But, before I take you home, we should take one last stroll around the city. What do you say?" He held out his arm to me.

"As long as it involves coffee and being with you, then I say yes."

"Oh. I see coffee comes before me. Thanks, Gi," he teased.

We had a lovely walk through the city, arms linked. The city is usually scorching in the summer, but today there were cool breezes. I asked him what he thought of Kansas, you, Donny, Mama, Papa, and Tom.

"I like it on the farm. The city's nice and all, but I suppose I'm a country boy at heart." Then he raised an eyebrow at me. "Gi, I honestly don't know why you left there. Your parents are wonderful people. Your Mama treated me like some long lost son. She would say, 'Willoughby, dear, you will be home for supper, won't you?' Then I'd come back from work to a house that smelled better than any restaurant or cafe in New York. She'd also slip cookies into my coat pockets, too. I'd be out working and then suddenly find a stash of oatmeal cookies in my pockets." He laughed.

"Sweet Mama," I said with a smile. "I miss her. I'm very glad she likes you, Will. What about … Papa?"

"When I first stepped into your house, Donny was sick, and your father wasn't in a cordial mood at all. I don't blame him. But I thought he hated me because he just kept glaring at me the whole night. We didn't talk until the next evening on the porch. He asked me who exactly I was. I told him I was a friend of his lovely daughter, Gi. He huffed a little bit. He said something like, 'She better not be makin' acquaintances with men in that blasted city.' And I said, 'I wholeheartedly agree.' He seemed a little surprised by my remark. We got on real well from then on."

"And what about Bess, Donny, and Tom?"

"I'm really fond of your siblings, Gi. I haven't seen mine in so long that it was nice to pretend they were mine, you know? Donny is a character. I'd be working on an interview, and he'd come up to me, asking if I wanted to race him in the fields. Gi, I can't turn down a race, even if I have pressing work to do. Gosh darn it, that kid would ask me every evening to race, and I barely got my assignments finished. You know what he said to me before I left?"

"Couldn't guess," I said.

"He said that he wished I would become his brother."

I blushed so much that for a moment I thought the fever had returned. "Oh! Donny is such a silly boy!" I laughed. "Now tell me about Bess and Tom."

"Oh those two," he smirked. "A match made in heaven if you ask me. Bessie is gentle, sweet, and steadfast in her responsibilities. Tom is adventurous and enjoys teasing her. He's a good kid, Gi. A real good kid. He brings out the best in her, and she in him. Neither of them know this, but your father caught on that they like each other. He called me out onto the porch one afternoon to talk to me about it. He wanted to know my opinion about those two. I said, 'Tom and Bessie go together like coffee and cream'. Your father was glad to hear it."

Will suddenly stopped walking, and I looked around, wondering what caused him to stop. All I could see were the carriage rides that cost a fortune to ride on. Will was fishing in his pocket for money. Then he walked over to a man in charge of the rides!

"Will!" I said. "What are you doing?"

"Come on, Gi! It's our last day in New York. Doesn't it seem right to take a carriage ride around Central Park?"

"I thought you told me to stay out of Central Park."

"Well, you didn't listen, did you?"

"No, I suppose I didn't. And I'm sorry for it."

He grabbed my hand and helped me up into the carriage. "All's forgiven," he said.

The seats were wonderfully cushy, and I snuggled deep into them, feeling like a queen. Then I reached forward and gently stroked the white horse who would be our escort. Will sat down next to me with a grin that just wouldn't go away. He seemed so cheerful and excited. I was extremely thrilled to be going on a carriage ride, but I didn't expect him to be quite so enthralled as I.

There was a reason behind his excited nature. And I didn't see it coming because I have a thick skull.

The carriage lurched forward as the horse started trotting. I grabbed Will's arm and let out a little screech, and he laughed at me. A breeze tossed my hair around, as I took in the beauty of the green trees and vivid flowers growing in Central Park.

"Oh, I forgot to give you the book I purchased yesterday," he said, reaching into his pocket. He presented it to me with bright eyes.

I held the beautiful copy in my hands, running my fingers across the smooth cover. "This is my favorite book, Will."

"I know."

I noticed a bookmark slipped right inside the book. I cracked it open, and my heart skipped a beat. No, two beats. Maybe even three. The bookmark was made of a light blue ribbon with ... with a *ring* tied to the end! I couldn't breathe, Bess. I honestly couldn't breathe. Then I saw Will's handwriting on the inside cover. It read:

July 1st, 1936

My darling Gi,

I've never read this book, but I heard from Bessie that you're similar to a Miss Jo March ... stubborn, spirited and adventurous. Georgiana Alexandria Rowland, you coming to New York City wasn't a mistake. God had something up his sleeve that I think we're both now seeing. Or perhaps we've always known, but didn't have the courage to say anything.

Gi, I want to spend the rest of my life with you. Will you marry me?

All my love,
Will

I stared at the words, my heart thudding inside me. I couldn't comprehend them. Will was asking me to marry him? Then, in an instant, I grabbed the pen that was sticking out of his coat pocket. In large letters I wrote:

Dearest Will,
YES, YES, YES!!!!
Your soon to be wife,
Gi

Then I lifted my eyes, and our gaze locked like before. Only this time, I didn't run.

"Will, I love you," I said.

He grinned. "And I love you, Gi."

Then I started jumping up and down in my seat, my cheerful disposition back in full function. "Will! We're getting married!" Of course he already knew that, but I felt the need to shout it in his face.

"Did you hear that?" Will shouted to the people in the streets. *"We're getting married!"*

A few people looked at us oddly, but we didn't care! I turned to Will and said, "Georgiana Reeves. That sounds nice, doesn't it?"

"Better than nice."

Then we both remembered the ring. He untied it from the ribbon and then held my hand as he slipped the silver band on my finger.

"Thanks for coming back for me," I said, twisting the ring on my finger. It felt *so right.*

"I couldn't let you go that easily."

"Is it true that you were on the same page of *Oliver Twist* for four months because you were staring at me? Or that you skipped meals to buy me things?"

He raised a brow. "How did you know that?"

"Mrs. West."

He shook his head with a little smirk. "She promised not to say anything."

"Well? Is it true?"

"Yeah. It's true."

"You're so sweet, Will." I leaned my head on his shoulder.

Then Will reached into his pocket and handed me a letter. "Almost forgot about this. I wrote to your parents, asking for their blessing. Your father wrote back. Want to read what they said?"

I unfolded the letter and eagerly ate up its contents.

Willoughby,

You have no idea how hard it is to give up your baby girl. I'm not so good at expressing myself, but I love that girl of mine. I had trouble letting her go to school, even though it was just down the road. I had trouble letting her visit friends, or go hiking and swimming by herself … I had trouble letting her go anywhere. So when she got this notion to live in New York, I was beside myself. But I couldn't stop her. We parted after a heated argument. I was angry at her, and I was sure she hated me. But neither of us would give in and be reconciled. If you ever wondered where Gi gets her stubborn streak, it's from me.

I always dreaded the thought of giving my daughters away in marriage. I was adamant that no man was good enough for my girls. But then a strange thing happened. You and Tom came along, and I began to take notice. I've been watching the way Tom treats Bess, and I was watching the way you talked about Gi. Even I saw the way your face beamed whenever she was brought up in conversation. And then I received your letter recounting the robberies and the reason for your sudden trip to New York. I believe that you will take good care of my daughter. You already have. I know you really love her. Her mama and I give our blessing for you two to be married. But please, bring her home.

– Humphrey Rowland

Bess, tears were running down my face. I feel so horrible for all the pain I caused Papa and Mama! I wished I could hug them right then and beg for their forgiveness!

Will looked down at me. "Ready to go home, Gi?"

"More than ready."

"And about that photography job ... have you changed your mind?"

I grinned at him. "I'll take it."

"Splendid."

And then I kissed him.

I've surrendered, Bess. I'm done with managing my life on my own. It doesn't work, and it's exhausting. I'm handing it over to God, and I'm going to stop running away from His plans for my life. Bess, I'm coming home. After I've arrived, and you've finished scolding me for being such a fool, will you help me plan my wedding? You will be my maid of honor, won't you?

Will and I will be home soon!

– Gi

July 7th, 1936

Oh, darling Gi!

I don't know what to say. I'm beside myself with excitement and happiness. I feel like ... I feel like Amy did, when she came home from Europe with her new husband on her arm and a family to whom she might return. Except I have considerably less grace than Amy. And I'm definitely more clumsy.

Gi, it rained.

Oh, let me begin at the beginning.

It was early in the morning on the Fourth. The windows were thrown open to let the cool morning air soak the house. I was in the kitchen, tying my hair up with two white hair ribbons. I was clad in my new pink frock, and eggs were boiling on the stove top when the screen door creaked and slammed, indicating Tom's arrival.

"Hello!" I called, frowning and untying the ribbon again because it felt like a mess. I threw them on the counter, deciding to forget them.

"Hey!" he called back, popping his head into the kitchen and grinning. "Happy Fourth!" He suddenly seized my hand, dragging me outside. "I've got somethin' for you."

He left me on the front porch, and I squinted from the early morning sunlight. "What on earth are you doing?" I cried suddenly, as Tom produced something from his pocket, struck a match, lit the object, and then threw it into the road.

It exploded.

I screamed. First it was from fear, and then it was from sheer excitement. "I love the Fourth!" I giggled.

Donny burst through the front door, his short legs running as fast as they could. "Firecracker!" he shouted. "Do it again, Tom!"

Tom laughed. "Can't. Grampa said I have to save the rest for when it gets dark out."

"Drat," Donny exclaimed, and it sounded hysterical coming from his little mouth. "Will you race with me?" he asked Tom.

Tom scratched his head, looking at me. Then, "Oh, okay." And the two charged into the field where I first found Tom on that cold winter's night.

It's fascinating how many very wonderful and very awful things can happen in so short a time.

Mama packed us all a lunch for the picnic. Boiled eggs, slices of bread, jars of milk, and cheese. Tom and his grampa provided soda crackers and sardines. (Don't worry, I didn't eat the sardines. That would be disgusting.)

The six of us walked to town. I was barefoot.

The picnic was to be held on the church lawn. Mrs. Harvey was already there, volunteering to help with the pies. Did I tell you about the pies? It was a bring-and-exchange deal. Several of the ladies baked pies and set them out on a table. Then you could bring something in exchange for a pie. Something useful, for Mrs. Harvey had told of the terrible Hoovervilles, and the church decided to give some things to the people in our own town's Hooverville. I asked Tom if that was charity. He hesitated before saying slowly, "Yes, I suppose so."

"Are the people going to accept it, then? Won't they get angry?"

Tom rubbed his chin, thinking. "Perhaps we could work out a deal with them—let them work for it somehow."

"The church needs painting," I pointed out.

Tom grinned. "You've got it, Hiccup." Then he went to speak to Reverend Wilkins.

I exchanged two old books for a pie. *The Pilgrim's Progress* and *Anne of Green Gables*. One of the ladies almost didn't let me. She said the items were meant to be useful, and she didn't see how reading material was physically useful for the homeless. "Yes, ma'am," I said in reply, "but they're emotionally useful. Sometimes words are life, ma'am, and maybe reading is what someone needs for encouragement right now."

I didn't realize Tom was standing behind me at the time. That is, until he started applauding after I finished my sentence. The lady laughed and said she saw my point, so she took the books and gave me an apple pie. Which I gave to Tom.

"For me?"

"Yeah," I said. "I don't like apples."

I do, actually. But I clammed up and didn't want to tell him I was planning on giving him the pie all along. I lied, Gi. I felt awful. But soon I forgot about it, in the flurry of the moment.

We ate our lunch under a scrubby old tree. The air was very hot, and I was sweating right through my pink frock, which was embarrassing. However, someone pulled out a fiddle. Tom's foot began tapping to the music. Papa laughed as Tom suddenly sprang up, whipping his hand toward me. "May I have this dance, mademoiselle?" he begged.

I smiled but said, "I can't. Doctor Murray said I can't do anything to strain my foot. And *your* dances are always straining." I laughed, leaning back against the tree trunk and taking another sip of milk.

Tom's grin faded slightly, but then he dragged Mama into a dance. She laughed and protested, but then we all discovered she's actually a very good dancer. We applauded her as she sat back down when it was over, out of breath. "Mama's good," Donny announced, and Mama laughed, kissing his cheek. Papa kissed *her* cheek.

Then Mama and I packed up the picnic basket. "Where'd Tom go?" I asked, looking around.

Mr. Thomas grinned slyly. "Talkin' to the fiddler, I reckon."

He was. I saw him talking earnestly to him, and I wondered what he was up to. I started to ask Mr. Thomas when the fiddler began playing a slower song. I'd say a waltz, but I'm not certain if that's what it was. All I know is the liveliness ceased, and a sweet, slow melody began. It was beautiful.

Then Tom showed up at my side and gently held out his hand. "A slow dance to accompany your weak ankles, ma'am." He used his wheedling tone.

I blushed intensely, I think, and said softly, "Okay."

So he swept me into a slow, quiet dance that didn't strain my ankle in the least. In fact, he held me so close I could have leaned my head against his chest and fallen asleep. And he wouldn't have let me fall. But I didn't do that. Instead, I said, "Priss has gotten big, hasn't she?"

"Yeah," he said, but his mind seemed elsewhere.

I was silent again a moment, listening to his breathing. Then I said, "This is a nice song."

"Yeah," he said again. Then he leaned down and whispered, "Bess."

"Yeah?" My stomach suddenly exploded into a million butterflies.

Then we heard a rumble of thunder. We looked at each other in surprise. I looked toward the horizon just as the sun was devoured by a light rain cloud. I started smiling, and my smile grew wider and wider as a drop of rain landed on my cheek. Then another dotted my arm, and all of a sudden it came down in torrents. I shrieked in laughter. "Look!" I cried, as if Tom couldn't see it. "Look! It's rain! It's actually raining!"

"Well, I'll be," he whispered and suddenly twirled me around. I leaned back and felt the delicious raindrops rolling down my neck. They were cool and gentle, and the breeze that blew chilled my bones in a way that felt glorious.

I suddenly grew very dizzy from the spinning, and the next thing I knew I had stumbled out of Tom's arms and tumbled to the ground. It knocked the breath out of me, and my new dress had a big brown scar across the hem.

Tom knelt down next to me, exclaiming, "I'm so sorry, Bess. I'm so, so sorry. Did you hurt your ankle again? Good Lord, I hope not."

I gave a short laugh. Then I laughed harder and harder until I couldn't control myself. I clutched my stomach and couldn't stand up. Tom stared at me. He grinned, his pale blue eyes glistening. When I had calmed, he stood up and held out his hands. I let him pull me out of the mud. Then we were dancing a slow dance again, nevermind the fact that the fiddler had gone away to get his fiddle out of the rain.

"Bess," Tom whispered as the rain poured down, soaking his hair until it dripped around his ears.

"Tom," I whispered back, breaking into a smile.

Then he took my face in both of his hands, staring at me. We stopped. "I love you," he whispered ardently.

"I—" I stopped, breathing. I closed my eyes. I wanted to live in that moment. I reached up and touched his forearms, clutching them tightly. I took a deep breath and breathed in the smell of rain on dry earth, the sound of pattering droplets that sprinkled the world, and the certain wanderlust I had felt but never expressed before. I felt his rough hands on my hot cheeks, and my eyelids fluttered open, finding his pale blue eyes fixed tenderly upon my face. Those dear, darling blue eyes.

"Bess?"

"Yeah?"

"I love you." There was anxiety hiding in his eyes now, and I felt a pang as I realized he began to doubt that I felt the same. I couldn't do to him as his mother did to my father. And I knew why.

I loved him.

I did something pretty foolish then. Actually, I suppose it wasn't foolish. Rash, yes. Foolish, no. I rose up on my toes and kissed his chin. "I love you too," I said softly.

His familiar smile flashed then. His blue eyes rose with a wild-like joy, and he picked me up by the waist and spun me around. "I love you," he laughed. It was as if a smile wasn't enough to express his happiness, and only pure laughter would do.

I laughed too, and I threw my arms around his neck, squeezing him tightly.

The sun broke out from behind a cloud, but the rain still poured down. It sparkled in the sudden sunlight. "I bet there'll be a rainbow," Tom said, setting me on my feet. The mud squelched between my toes, and it was a beautiful feeling.

Suddenly there was a loud explosion, and I jumped. Tom and I turned toward the sound, and we found Mr. Thomas grinning sheepishly by the old tree. Donny held a half-burnt match in his chubby fingers, and his eyes were wide with excitement and wonder.

"Donny!" I shouted. I broke away from Tom and tore the match out of Donny's little fingers a moment later. An exploded firecracker lay not far away. "Mr. Thomas, how could you? He's barely six years old!" I scolded, taking Donny in my arms and kissing his cheeks.

"Sorry, ma'am," Mr. Thomas said meekly, and Tom tried to hide the smile on his face.

And that's how Donny almost died. Again.

That evening, after the firecrackers had been lit (by Tom this time), and the pies had been eaten, Mama was putting Donny to bed. Papa was indoors reading the paper, I think, and Mr. Thomas had gone home. Tom and I sat on the front porch. I swung my legs gently, looking up at the night sky. It was clear. You could still smell the sweet smell of moisture soaking into the earth, but the rain had stopped. The stars were intensely bright that night, and the moon was full.

Tom and I were mesmerized.

"It's like flying," I murmured, pointing toward the moon.

Tom slipped his arm around me. "Yeah," he said, nudging me and pointing toward the American flag hanging from his front porch across the road. "And being set free."

I smiled and stood up. I grabbed his hand, and I led him to the tree. We both climbed up and crawled onto the porch roof. From there, we could see the little town in the distance. I pointed to the church steeple and the little cross upon the top of it.

His eyes glistened. "Yeah," he said softly. "That's being set free."

We stood on the porch roof for awhile, just breathing and thinking and living. Then Tom said, "I better go home now."

"Yeah," I said. "Me too."

So he climbed down the tree first, and I climbed down after him. He squeezed my hand, smiling at me, before shoving his hands in his pockets and striding across the road to his house. He paused at the front door to look back at me. I waved. Then he went inside.

I lingered a moment longer out-of-doors. It was so cool and beautiful out. And I felt contentment, not wanderlust. I turned to our house. The windows glowed yellow. It was the welcoming color of home. I bounded up the porch steps and found Papa in the living room, his head bent over a piece of paper. He looked up when I came in.

"Come here, pet," he said gently. I came, and he took me on his knee. He bent the crook of his head over mine like he did when I was little, and I leaned my head against his chest.

"You like Tom, don't you, sugar?"

I smiled. "Yeah. I reckon."

"You love him." It wasn't a question. It was a statement.

"Yeah," I whispered. "I reckon I do." I lifted my head. "You like him, Papa? Are you happy about it?"

Papa sighed deeply. "Yeah, hon'," he said at last, "I reckon I am. You gotta understand, though. It's ... tough."

"I understand."

"Y'do?"

"Yeah." I smiled, leaning my head against his chest again and kicking my feet against the arm of the chair. "I love you, Papa."

Silence. Then, "I love you too."

I was incandescently happy. Suddenly Papa handed me the piece of paper. It was a letter. "I got this a few days ago," Papa said. "And I replied."

It was Will's letter, explaining about you and the robberies. And then he asked for permission to marry you. I nearly had a heart attack of joy then. I froze and then sat up straight, squealing, "Oh, Papa! What did you say? Did you tell them yes? What will Gi say? Oh, Papa, does this mean she's coming home?" I was beside myself.

Papa was strangely solemn about the ordeal. "I gave him my blessing. I reckon she'll say yes." There was a pause. "She'd be a fool not to."

That's how I knew that Papa loves Will like a son. And that's how I knew that Papa misses you dreadfully.

Your letter filled me to the brim, Gi. "My cup runneth over." Yes, I'll be your maid of honor! Yes, I'll tell you you're a fool! Yes, I'll cover you with hugs and kisses on your return!

It's been seven months, Gi. And a most beautiful, God-filled seven months they have been.

"Thank God," Amy March declared at the end of the story. "I'm a happy woman."

And I am echoing her words today.

Tom and I are awaiting your return with Will.

Give him my love.

Ever your loving, little sister,

    Bess

Acknowledgements

When we first began writing the *Ain't We Got Fun* letters, the inspiration was derived partly from a fellow blogger and partly from a forgotten idea that had been abandoned a year before. The blogger being a young woman named Rachel Heffington and the idea that had been ours alone.

All of this to say, even from the very beginning, *Ain't We Got Fun*'s very existence depended on the help and encouragement of one another and other very important persons in our lives.

Thank you to our blog readers. Without you, it is unlikely these would have been compiled into a published work. Your eagerness to read the letters and your encouragement have been a huge blessing. Your responses blew us away, and we are beyond thankful to those who were the First Readers.

Thank you to our dear editor, Maria Putzke. You were such a help in getting this work into tip-top shape, and we are very grateful.

Thank you to Rachel Rossano, for creating such a beautiful cover and making our whole book look pretty, inside and out. Thank you for being so patient! We'd recommend your work to anyone.

And, in an awkward way, it is one another that we ought also to thank. This was entirely a twosome endeavor, and we couldn't have done it if we had not worked together as a team.

Most importantly, we thank You, Jesus, for giving us this priceless opportunity to share You through innocent stories that attempt to humbly portray life and lives the way they are. "But God forbid that I should boast except in the cross of our Lord Jesus Christ, by whom the world is crucified to me, and I to the world." – Galatians 6:14

Also by Emily Chapman:

1620 – When a voyage to the New World is thrust upon young Hope Ellison, her carefully built ideals begin to slip from her grasp. Clinging to the tattered shards of her once contented life, she embarks on the perilous journey with her family, caring not for the reason they are taking such risks in the first place and fearing the fate for her future. Yet, even her fears are unprepared for the trials ahead, and soon she comes face to face with choices that will define her view of life entirely.

Cry of Hope is available in paperback on Amazon.com.

Also by Emily Ann Putzke:

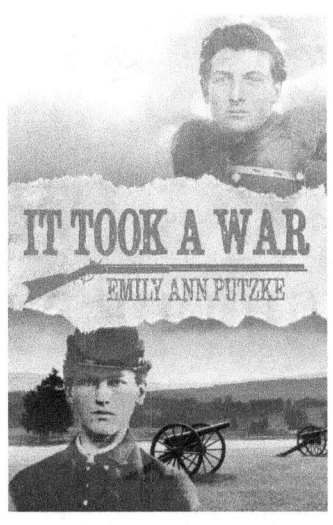

1861 – Sixteen year old Joe Roberts leads a mundane life as far as he's concerned. His world spins in the same circle each day: working at his family's store, taking his sisters on boyish escapades and bickering with his rogue of a cousin, Lucas. Joe can't understand why his mother allows Lucas to live and work with them after all the pain he caused their family. When war is declared, Joe is quick to join up and become a soldier with the 11th Pennsylvania Volunteers, but war is nothing like he imagined. To make matters worse, he must endure having Lucas in the same regiment. Can Joe put the pain of the past behind him? Forgiveness is easier said than done.

It Took a War is available in paperback, kindle, and audiobook on Amazon.com.

EMILY CHAPMAN, also known as Bess Rowland, is a young hobbit living in the dear old South, and she is entirely bonkers. She's a dreamer, an optimistic pessimist, and an introverted people person. Blue skies, dancing, Disney, and whipped cream make her happy, and she swears she's once been to Narnia. She's been a reader all her life, became a writer because of that, and published her first novel, *Cry of Hope*, in March of 2014. But without her Savior, all of this would mean nothing. It is in Him that she puts her hope.

You can learn more about Emily Chapman and her books at www.emilychapmanauthor.com and www.facebook.com/emilychapmanauthor.

EMILY ANN PUTZKE and Gi Rowland have two big things in common: their love for God and coffee. Besides writing historical fiction, Emily enjoys being an aunty, photography, Irish dancing, spending time with family, attempting to play the guitar, reenacting, and reading. She loves polka dots, war movies, and all things vintage. Her first novella, *It Took a War*, was published in December of 2014.

You can learn more about Emily Ann Putzke and her books at www.authoremilyannputzke.com and www.facebook.com/authoremilyannputzke.